BENJAMIN MYERS was born in Durham in 1976. His most recent novel *The Offing* was a bestseller. Other works include *The Gallows Pole*, which won the Walter Scott Prize for historical fiction, and *Beastings*, which was awarded the Portico Prize for Literature. *Pig Iron* won the inaugural Gordon Burn Prize, while *Richard* was a *Sunday Times* Book of the Year. He has also published non-fiction, poetry and crime novels, while his journalism has appeared in publications including the *Guardian*, *New Statesman*, *Spectator*, *Caught By The River* and many more.

@benmyers1

ALSO BY THE SAME AUTHOR

Fiction
The Offing
These Darkening Days
The Gallows Pole
Turning Blue
Beastings
Pig Iron
Richard

Non-fiction
Under The Rock

MALE TEARS

BENJAMIN MYERS

BLOOMSBURY PUBLISHING
LONDON · OXFORD · NEW YORK · NEW DELHI · SYDNEY

BLOOMSBURY PUBLISHING
Bloomsbury Publishing Plc
50 Bedford Square, London, WC1B 3DP, UK
29 Earlsfort Terrace, Dublin 2, Ireland

BLOOMSBURY, BLOOMSBURY PUBLISHING and the Diana logo
are trademarks of Bloomsbury Publishing Plc

First published in Great Britain 2021
This edition published 2022

Copyright © Benjamin Myers, 2021

A catalogue record for this book is available from the British Library

ISBN: HB: 978-1-5266-1135-2; TPB: 978-1-5266-1134-5; EBOOK: 978-1-5266-1132-1;
PB: 978-1-5266-1136-9; EPDF: 978-1-5266-4289-9

2 4 6 8 10 9 7 5 3 1

Typeset by Integra Software Services Pvt. Ltd
Printed and bound in Great Britain by CPI Group (UK) Ltd, Croydon CR0 4YY

MIX
Paper from
responsible sources
FSC® C171272

To find out more about our authors and books visit www.bloomsbury.com
and sign up for our newsletters

Contents

The tragedy of machismo is that a man is never quite man enough.

—Germaine Greer

A Thousand Acres of English Soil

The hare is on its haunches and sniffing the air when the man enters the middle field. It watches from a distance with its ears tilted to the breeze and then when the man stumbles on the rutted edge of soil it turns and runs away at half-speed.

The man sees the white smudge of its rump bouncing over stubble. He has always thought it nature's cruel irony to place a target on such a stealthy creature; a mark of imperfection to prevent it evolving beyond its capabilities.

He pauses and watches as the hare takes long strides towards the safety of the hedgerow's shadows at the far edge of the field, the taut sinews of its legs flexing.

He has been raised to believe that the sighting of the season's first hare is symbolic, though he cannot remember for certain whether it represents good or ill fortune. As a man of the soil and the woods and the holloways, his inclination is towards the latter. He reads the hare as a portent.

The man walks the field's perimeter and enjoys the low-slung sun on his face. He watches the lazy beginnings of its day-long arc across the field, and he feels glad for the first time this year that he can walk to work. Other farmers would think him odd to spend a single extra second outdoors, and often in autumn and winter he curses the mile-and-a-half walk that takes him along the old railway track, under the bridge and up on to the new cycle path, recently laid from a useless granular mix that holds puddles like a thirsty man cups cold water from a farmyard spigot on a hot harvesting day.

On dark damp mornings when he needs a torch to avoid these sump pools, or in winter when the frost is stretched tight over the ground and a cruel wind cuts across the open field and gets beneath his layers, he would rather be anywhere else. But today he does not mind because like the hare he can smell the incoming season on the breeze.

Walking this way connects him to the past. He is following a carved niche, a route – a tradition – that is centuries old.

The dry spell means that the lane linking the middle field to the storage barns is hardened and the soil already webbed with a matrix of cracks. The deep furze that lines the lane briefly blocks the sun but then the ground is solid underfoot and he is walking across the yard to unlock the bolt. He takes a key and opens a padlock that secures the double doors of the larger of the two corrugated barns, then feeds a long thick chain through his cold hands.

The man opens one sturdy door and turns on the light. He deactivates the alarm. He thinks he hears the light skittering of claws on concrete and the sound of something – the discarded metal lid of a tin of paint, perhaps – being nudged a fraction of an inch. A short, sharp scraping.

The picker is parked half in darkness like a great sleeping beast, but when the man opens up the second door and the sun shines in to illuminate the full brilliance of its red paintwork, it is almost as if the beast stirs, as if it is coming alive with a sigh after a lengthy slumber. The machine makes him think of mythical creatures; lumbering monstrosities as seen in childhood books. Dragons and gryphons and phoenixes made mechanical.

Every morning he feels dwarfed by its presence and quietly in awe of the ten thousand components that have gone into creating this piece of equipment more intricate and complex than a human skeleton.

The man takes out his key fob and climbs into the cab. He starts the motor. He feels the automated vibrations rising through the core of him.

––––

The boy picked his way down the dirt bank using tiny sidesteps. Plastic. There was plastic everywhere: poking up through the soil like fresh shoots and tangled amongst ancient and complicated roots.

He skidded but then corrected himself, and turned the other way like a skier traversing the lower slopes of the Eiger.

He should have been at school but instead he was outdoors in the green cathedral of the old wood. Here was where he felt he was learning things, things that mattered about growth and life and the inevitability of death. Next to such a subject, the study of arithmetic and long-buried monarchs felt like a worthless distraction.

The old town tip sat in a now-neglected clearing in the wooded hillside, where nature and man's discarded items appeared to be locked in permanent battle. Refuse once dumped from flatbed trucks and skips, and pulled from boot and barrow to be flung into a vast pit two or three decades earlier then buried beneath a scattering of soil, was slowly rising to the surface. Decades of rain had washed away the loam to reveal a layer of lives once led: a legacy of household waste blooming like a grotesque bed of bouquets. Of broken china and old beer cans with branding now outdated, and glass bottles with stoppers instead of caps. The boy saw twists of tarpaulin sheeting and the occasional shoe.

Other times it appeared as if the soil was swallowing everything, sucking it under like quicksand. Certainly the filled-in mineshafts that had been known to collapse here showed that the ground was capable of movement, that it was a porous and amorphous entity with a life of its own. That was why the wood was now deemed a danger and permanently fenced off to the public.

This space belonged to the nettles and the ivy now. The woods belonged to the balsam and the ragwort and the animals.

The boy had seen deer and foxes up in here. He had seen a pair of nesting ravens, owls, dozens of squirrels and rabbits, and once, at dusk, a badger. Most commonplace were the rats that nested in the fissures and hollows of the tip. First attracted by dumped vats of school kitchen fat and rotten butcher's offal, they now thrived in a kingdom rarely visited by humans.

There were still things to be found by those few who looked for them, artefacts from a changing world. Old clocks and jam jars and marbles, and pram wheels that the boy could use to build a bogie with, or clothes horses and rusted bike chains to wield as weapons, or tea trays for when it snowed. A box under his bed held his treasures. Coins and beads and a large penknife, its blade blunted and mottled green.

The boy went down to the tip's far corner. He used a stick to prod and turn the soil. He saw coiled springs and matted clothes with floral patterns and broken buttons. He saw more bottles, upended. They made him think of ostriches.

He stepped between the plastic pieces of things once functional, now cracked and scattered, and a pile of newspapers wadded into a pulpy slab the size of a pillow, its colours rain-run and the words blurred into history. There were bags of ballast containing concrete hardened into strange sculptural contortions. Rubber Marigold gloves and roof slates. Twisted tyres. Spent aerosols. Cracked crockery and warped Tupperware tubs. A spool of police crime-scene tape. A skein of cable.

Something about the shape of a dull and rusted piece of metal sticking from the soil drew the boy closer. When he pushed on it with his foot it gave a little, but his pump came loose and he had to tie his lace. He levered it again and it gave some more. It appeared to be part of something greater; a component. But when he got both hands around it and hefted it from the soil as if he were pulling up carrots, it suddenly came loose and he had to take backward steps.

The boy turned it over. He saw that it had jaws. The jaws had teeth and the teeth were locked into place, and the boy was glad. There was a pin hanging loose and a flat piece of metal beneath the jaws. It was all held together by a frame.

There was something malevolent about the contraption. Years in the soil had not robbed it of its potential for violence. The boy felt in danger just holding it in his hands while alone there in the wood. But he felt excited too.

———

A thousand acres surround the man and the picking is good. The potatoes come up easy and he sees that it is to be his season. A time of plenty. Blight destroyed the crop last year – turned it into an infected mush that he wouldn't even put in a hog trough – but now the elements are working his way.

Last week it was raining stair rods and just yesterday there were clouds scudding so low that the man was sure there was going to be another downpour so violent that it would leave the vast potato tracts sodden. But the sky held and now he sits atop the machine as it crawls spider-like across the field.

The potato picker does the labour of eighteen men. That was how many were in the team when his father first worked these fields fifty years ago and would come home exhausted, falling asleep during his first roll-up. Now most potato farmers plough and till and harvest alone, working wordlessly like solitary sailors adrift on their expansive inland oceans of dirt.

The man works the control panel, continually checking buttons and reading meters to make sure that his line stays true and remains flush with the edge of the field. Coordinates on a touchscreen GPS map guide him.

The machine growls and purrs and whirs as mechanical side-fingers comb the earth like a plough on an ox's yoke, but so much faster and neater and without blisters or strained muscles. Twin elevators scoop, sieve and separate the potatoes. A push of a button carries them up by rubber conveyor belt into the heart of the red metallic beast, rolling them out the back into a bunker with a six-tonne storage capacity. Pebbles and small stones and clods are filtered away through webs while the screen feeds the man statistics concerning his bounty. Storage capacity used. Net weight. Yield.

Beneath him unseen threshing blades top the haulm.

Once, a topper would have to be fixed on to the front of the tractor and pushed through the potato patches, but not any more. The big red beast does that too. And afterwards, when the work is done, the machine will fold its limbs away. The push of another button will see components retract and return, compactly stowed.

The machine is worth more than the average family home.

Seeing thousands of mud-pocked potatoes bobbing and rolling up the belt is hypnotic to him. Trance-inducing. He sees them as people. He sees them as heads. They make him think of airports and train platforms and London at rush hour.

The sun is up now, and there is a bee trapped in his cab but it does not bother him so he does not bother it. He lets it idly bat against the glass and leans an elbow out of the window, watching the rolling potatoes and feeling the low sonorous rumble of the shifting of his harvest in the storage chamber, the sound of organic matter on metal. Today there is no better noise.

The man reaches the end of row number three and takes the corner wide, sees the camber of the field sloping to his right and the sun climbing higher still, and he locks into the ritual of the centuries.

———

The boy waited until later to ask his father what it was. He was sure he knew already, but he needed confirmation.

After tea, with a brew and a burn-up blazing in the smoke-blackened fireplace, was the time to approach him.

His father had been out in the fields all day and already his chin was sinking to his chest.

'Dad. Do you know what this is?'

His father looked up at him with eyes rimmed red from twelve hours in the billowing clouds of dusty chaff, and for a moment he just stared at his son as if he wasn't there, and then he blinked and held out his hand.

The boy passed him the locked lump of rust.

His father took it and turned it. He scraped at the rust with the rounded end of his teaspoon handle.

'That's a gin trap, is that,' he said.

'Gin trap?'

'That's what they call them. *Gin* is short for *engine*.'

The boy wiped his nose with the back of his hand.

'They made them from forged steel,' said his father. 'Where did you get this?'

'From the tip.'

'They're illegal. And I told you not to go up there.'

'Why are they illegal?'

His father put his cigarette down. He ran his fingers over the metal teeth and then tried to prise the jaws apart.

'Needs oiling.'

'Why are they illegal, Dad?'

9

'Changing attitudes,' he said. 'They weren't always banned. Time was, all gamekeepers and farmers would have a brace of these about the place – those that wanted the rabbits kept out their patches, that is. The blacksmith would make them up. They used to be as common as turnips, did the old gin traps.'

'Is that what they're used for, then – bagging rabbits?'

'Mainly, though they'd catch anything that cared to cross them. But then folk started keeping rabbits as pets. They got soft over them and began moaning about things they knew nothing about. You know what they're like, the town folk and that lot in the new-builds. Them on the estates.'

His father scowled as he said this. Any mention of the estates angered him and whenever the word came from his mouth he would tip his head towards the new houses that had been built half a mile away; a place the boy was being raised to view with suspicion, disdain and bitterness. *The estates* was a curse worse than any other.

Because the new homes with their trimmed lawns and streets that went nowhere but back in on themselves surely signalled the slow death of agriculture. According to his father they were one more kick in the teeth for the farmers whose plots were being carved up and sold off to be buried beneath tarmac and asphalt.

'How long since they were used?'

His father picked up his cigarette and inhaled, then rested it back on the lip of the ashtray.

'Ten or twenty years since, I reckon. The fifties.'

'Is it worth anything?' asked the boy.

His father handed it back. 'Probably about fifty per cent of nothing. Chuck it.'

'Do you reckon we can get it working?'

'You don't want to be messing with that. You'll get hurt.'

'We could leave it on the estate,' said the boy.

His father reached for his cigarette and smiled at this. It was a thin, diluted smile, but a rare smile all the same. He sat back in his armchair.

'Go and fetch us the oilcan and a rag from the shed,' he said. 'And bring my mallet.'

———

Gulls follow the picker, dipping for worms. They hang suspended, jostling in the mid-air before taking it in turns to swoop down.

Great elongated strands hang squirming from their beaks as they bank upwards and away, and then the next clustered phalanx of screeching birds descend.

The sea is thirty miles away, yet still they come.

The man does not notice them. He is watching his dials and smoking a roll-up that he holds between two yellowed fingers on his left hand. The other he dangles out the window. If the weather holds, by harvest end his arms will be berry-brown and covered in a down of hairs bleached blonde by the sun. A true farmer's tan.

He lets the beast do all the work as it greedily snatches and sorts the potatoes from the pitted clod. They are Maris Pipers: the best you can get. He will get top price for Pipers and in late September he will go somewhere far from here.

After he clears the tenth turn the man allows himself the luxury of letting his mind wander. He pictures a restaurant terrace overlooking the sea. Waves are breaking gently on the shore. There is a glass of beer. It is so cold that beads of condensation cling to it. He raises it and takes a sip. Drains it. Signals to the waiter for another.

The beast jolts and there is a noise that he implicitly knows is wrong. A judder then a coarse grinding that cuts through the low hum of the engine and the echoing rumble of the falling potatoes.

The man halts the machine but leaves it running in order to keep the programmed settings on course. He throws his roll-up and then climbs down from the cab. He sees the trail of gulls and then something – he thinks it is perhaps a rock – that is obstructing the blades on the nearside edge. Protruding from the soil, it is a small boulder that is not yet fully jammed and is near enough to get to.

The man crouches and then he lies down and draws his leg up. He kicks the rock and it shifts slightly. He bends at the knees and kicks harder this time but now it does not move. Looking up, he can see daylight through the machine. He can see a tranquil and clear blue sky shot through with a single vapour trail fattening and fading away into the distance.

He climbs into his cab and he gets a pitchfork and then he gets down beneath the machine and pokes and prods but the rock won't budge so he climbs around the side of the cab and on to the front of the machine. It is polished. Waxed pristine. The sun is glinting off it. The machine is beautiful. It purrs.

The man sees the rock in the haulm topper. He inverts the fork and jams it down and he hits the rock and it budges but as it does he slips and his centre of gravity is a nebulous thing because then something is snatching at the hem of his trousers. It jerks and pulls and he feels his foot being crushed and rolled like the last curl of a tube of toothpaste. The pain takes him to another planet.

Yet he is silent as he lifts his other leg and twists and turns in an attempt to free himself, but this just seems to pull him in deeper as the haulm-threshing blades eat up first one leg and then the other. The machine chews up his shins and thigh bones and the man is screaming now, and squirming too, and then a guard rail drops down and the blades slow to a half-speed and then they stop and his legs are an elongated pulpy mess of muscle, string and sinew extending several feet deep into the belly of the beast.

The gulls hover high above him as he loses first blood and then consciousness.

The boy couldn't miss any more school so he rose early, quietly drank milk from the bottle and then took one of his father's Capstans. The birds were singing when he left the house, and the day was just a tiny torn streak across the hem of the darkened sky.

The oiled trap was wrapped up in an old rag that was tucked into the pit of his arm. A bread roll was in his pocket. He walked down empty streets and he whistled as the sun unfolded itself across the sky and the day was born as if for the very first time.

To rid the tip of rats would be doing the town a favour, he thought. One or two a day was a lot of rats, whichever way up you looked at it.

He climbed a fence and dropped into the still and silent wood.

As the boy approached the old tip, the air was heavy with a fugue-like haze and the trees were as tall as church spires.

He unwrapped the gin trap and crouched, hooking his thumb through the spring eye and then squeezing the sprung bar down. It took one foot to hold the device in place and all his strength to prise open the jaws. He used a rock to wedge it while he slotted the catch. Without taking his eye off the contraption he felt around for a stick, and when he found one the boy gently tapped the rusted base plate and – *snap*. He jumped as the jaws slammed shut and the stick sheared in two. The teeth locked tightly together.

The ferocity of the device's violence was alarming and thrilling. He wanted to see it in action again immediately so he did one more test run and then carefully baited it with bread and walked backwards in case his movements set it off a third time.

He sat back on a damp mattress and took out the cigarette. From here you could see through the trees to the patchwork of fields that his father worked further down the valley. The cigarette was bent but not broken. The boy lit it and inhaled. Coughed. He was still learning how to smoke and preferred to do it alone. Also it made him feel sick and dizzy. He smoked it halfway and then he carefully ground it out and pocketed what was left.

The boy watched the trap for a little longer. The wood was quiet and still, and though he wanted to lie back and stay here forever, he stood and stretched and reluctantly began the walk to school.

———————

The man wakes to silence and the sun on his face. The sun blinding him. There are no birds and his legs are ruined up to the thigh. They are shattered and matted and dripping.

Time becomes a new thing to consider now. It has been recalibrated to an abstract configuration based upon pain.

The man is shaking uncontrollably and he is cold and he feels stupid here, propped upright in the machine, like a piece of bread stuck in a toaster or an old bank statement fed into an office shredder. He hates himself for allowing this to happen. For manufacturing his own indignity.

Once, there would have been other men here. Labourers and pieceworkers. There would have been a team but now there is only a machine and the machine is controlling him and there is no one to hear his muted moans and dry heaves.

The man feels the thousand acres of English soil begin to rotate around him. He is the epicentre of a centrifugal force that is driving the landscape and driving the planet as the soil circles. He retches as something bitter splashes at the back of his throat. He tries to spit, but drools on his chin instead. Something wet hangs there for a moment before falling on to his work shirt.

To move an eyelid is to increase his suffering and to breathe is to plumb the depths of this wellspring of pain. But breathe he must, so this is what he focuses on: inhaling and then exhaling. It is the most complicated thing he has had to do in his life. Inhaling and then exhaling. Each breath is a century of pain but it does not hurt as much as the realisation that he may never be found; that the sun will move across the sky and day will become night and night will become day again, and there will be no one around to miss him and eventually he will rot and the machine will still be standing here in the middle of the field for decades, rusting into stasis, a relic for future days.

The gulls that seemed to disappear have now returned. The man can hear them behind him, first as they argue over worms and then more loudly when they are disturbed by a bullish crow that arrives amongst them like a black napkin blown in on the breeze.

The engine ticks over.

———————

Dusk had settled over the wood like a curtain falling.

The insistent reedy rattle of a far-off woodpecker tapped out a rhythm to echo up through the columns as the boy crossed the tip towards the trap.

The evening was perfectly still until something rounded appeared to rise before him, an ungainly thing ten yards away from where he had set the trap. It was a badger with its teeth bared.

The boy stopped and held his breath and then he found a stick and slowly walked towards it. The creature cowered and balled up. Its front right leg was caught between the jaws of the gin trap, close to its knee joint.

As he got closer the badger snittered. It was a diabolical sound of pure and concentrated fear.

There was blood around its maw. It was matted there. Tufted. With eyes open wide the badger tried to flee, but the trap anchored it to the soil and it could only awkwardly drag it. The boy saw a further trail of blood across the surface of the tip.

Only then did he notice the ragged wound below the teeth of the trap – much further down towards its foot. It could not have been caused by the trap. The boy looked again and he saw the blood and the sharp teeth and the badger's eyes and then he understood.

This wound was of its own making. In its desperation, the creature was trying to chew off its own paw. Deep in the hot wet redness of the self-inflicted wound that was the beginnings of an amputation, the boy could see bone.

He turned and ran and he kept running.

The sun has climbed the ladder of the sky and the man can feel his head burning under its glare. The itchiness of his scalp now bothers him more than his extirpated lower limbs.

He calculates it to be as close to midday as you can register without a watch.

Perhaps sensing a better feeding ground elsewhere – the man imagines a rising shoal of herring speckling the surface of the North Sea silver – the gulls have left him again and the field is silent.

He has not yet dared to look down but when he finally forces himself to he sees his waist is as normal, but beneath it through the gaps in the metal machinery there is a tattered dangling mess. He can see strings and blood and ribbons and no feet, and only then does the man remember the badger of his childhood.

Only then does he remember the look in the creature's eyes all those years ago, as it flapped and flailed in the dirt of the tip. And the noise it made: the howl of a cornered and fearful thing.

He hears it again as he opens up his lungs and the same howl rises high above him. Hears it trapped in the amber of the moment.

———

The father beat the boy and when the boy had stopped crying they took torches and walked in silence up to the road and then on to the back track. At night the wood wore a different mask; it was a haunted place alive with creaks and groans and the warning calls of beasts. Once, something loud exploded from the branches above them but it was gone before their beams could frame it. Later the boy thought he felt something brush lightly across his shins as he walked but he did not dare mention it.

He led his father down the slopes to the tip and when he reached it he pointed with his torch and right up until this last moment he still held hope that the creature would not be there – that it had managed to free itself or, better still, someone had freed it for them – and for a second it seemed like it had gone, but then the boy saw that it had dragged the trap back to where he had originally set it.

The badger was tired. The fight within it was fading, but their arrival galvanised it into one final flurry of panic as it slunk in retreat and made a piercing noise. It was a howl of terror accompanied by a frantic scratching at the earth.

Two metallic-blue eyes stared into the source of the light as his father put a hand firmly on the boy's chest and said: 'Wait here – and keep that beam on it.'

The boy did as he was told until his father raised the wrench high above his head and then he dropped the torch, and everything was darkness.

The Folk Song Singer

The sky is stretched tight across the city. It has a strange hue and there is a charge to the air. It is storm season and the clouds are moiling.

He arrives uncharacteristically early and takes a seat so that he can look down the street and watch her walk, can observe her without the pretence of the interview situation. He sits for a minute before deciding that perhaps she might not like being on display like that, like meat in a butcher's window, so he moves to a table further back, in the darker corner of the cafe.

He has crossed seven postcodes and one river to be here in West London. Unfamiliar territory.

The cafe was her publicist's suggestion. He had said it was just around the corner from her house and that she would feel at ease there. She did not do many interviews these days. She was, the publicist had said, nervous. *Reticent* was another word that was used.

The writer checks his notepad, checks his tape recorder. He orders coffee and a glass of water. He opens a packet of strong mints and tips one into his mouth but finds himself chewing it straight away and the sharp sugary chunks stick in his throat. He is coughing when the folk song singer arrives. He is swallowing water when she walks towards him.

She glides.

She is smaller in real life. In his experience they usually are – almost every pop star he has ever interviewed.

They shake hands awkwardly – he squeezing too hard and she flinching, retracting and then wordlessly retreating to the counter to order coffee.

————

She looks older than in those photographs so familiar to him. He should not be surprised – she has been out of the public eye for years. There have been no TV appearances and only the odd magazine retrospective around the time of a rare new release, usually a refor-matted album reissue. But her famed bone structure is still striking and her cobalt eyes the bluest he has seen. So chillingly blue he finds it hard to look directly at her.

She is wearing a nutmeg-coloured blouse and is swathed in silk scarves despite the mugginess of the August afternoon.

She is an attractive woman.

The writer wonders if she is attractive because it is her, the folk song singer whose music he has grown up on, whose voice defined an era, and whether that attraction comes merely from recognition and admiration in the same way that he once had a slightly unexpected crush on Germaine Greer after seeing her absent-mindedly tearing at a croissant in Brixton Market. Or is it simply because ageing can never fully wither a strong frame and good cheekbones – that it can crack the paint but not the canvas?

She rattles with bangles as she sits. The coffee follows her and she thanks the waiter by his first name. For a fleeting moment the writer experiences that disconnected sense of being faced with someone so utterly familiar yet completely unknown: an intimate stranger. For most of his life she has been a voice in a spiralling groove on old vinyl, and a half-dozen iconic promotional photos. An *Old Grey Whistle Test* clip on YouTube. Their relationship has been a one-way street – him consuming her – and now that strange sensation is creeping towards anxiety. It feels like fingers tapping at the underside of his sternum; a sharpening of the senses, yet a disarming mental blankness too.

The folk song singer puts on her glasses and looks at him, seeing him for the first time. Her expression is neutral and her earrings are a miniature set of peacock feathers. One on each side.

An extra set of eyes observing him.

'Congratulations on your new album,' he says, because he has to say something. His job is, of course, to initiate. 'I like it a lot.'

'Thank you. But you really don't have to say that.'

'No, I genuinely like it.'

She nods. 'You sound surprised at this discovery?'

'No, it's just that some old – '

He catches himself.

'I mean, when you've had as long a career as you – '

'It's not that long. Most of it is crammed into a little over a ten-year period.'

'The seventies?'

'More or less. Starting at the fag-end of the sixties and on into the early eighties.'

'It's interesting you say that because I was going to ask about when you wrote – '

'Let me just stop you there for a second because I think I know what comes next.'

'You do?'

'Yes. Do you know how many recorded songs I've sung on?'

'No. A lot, I imagine.'

'My publisher does. He tells me that it's two hundred and twenty-four. That includes singles, album tracks, other people's songs, backing vocals, jingles. Everything that warrants a mechanical royalty.'

'That's substantial.'

'It is substantial, yes. And do you know how many of those I get asked about?'

He demurs. 'Point taken.'

'One,' she continues. 'One song. "We Walk Through the Woodlands". That's what you were going to ask about, wasn't it? "We Walk Through the *bloody* Woodlands".'

He pauses for a moment to regroup his thoughts.

'Don't you think it's natural to want to ask about that song, though? It's practically the national anthem of the folk world; people will still be singing that in a hundred years' time. There are very few other songs I could say that about.'

'Well. Neither of us will ever know.'

'It must have been kind to you.'

'You mean financially?'

'Well, yes. Partly.'

'Possibly not as kind as you might think. I only have a co-credit.'

'But you've never had to – '

Again she interrupts him. 'Work? Well, I've never had a proper job like criticising people's music, if that's what you mean.'

———

They never change, she thinks. Not really. They are always male, for starters. Always. And of a certain disposition. Nervy and earnest. Keen to impress, yes, but their conversation always undercut with a streak of almost confrontational pedantry. They know facts and dates and session musicians and chart positions – the mental clutter of a patchwork career – that she has simply never bothered to memorise.

They still don't know how to dress themselves either. In a small concession towards formality she sees that the writer has put a shirt on, but it is creased and ill-fitting, fresh off a dismal studio-flat floor in a high-number postcode.

They live in their own worlds too, these jeans-and-T-shirt men. Music is their everything. And if not music, they would surely fixate on something else with the same obsessive devotion to completism and cataloguing. Fishing, cars, football. Pornography, perhaps. In her experience, all music journalists have shared a sense of fastidiousness.

They were like this back in the early seventies. Then, she endured a seemingly endless parade of them. They all smoked, they all grew out their beards and they were all of the left – as was she, but hopefully not to the point of caricature. The musicians were no different from the writers then either. They railed against greed and breadheads but sold one another out as soon as a cheque was dangled in front of them. They spoke out against homophobia and racism and oppression, then backhanded any women – their women, as ownership was always asserted and claims staked – that did them wrong. They trod all over them. Trampled them. But, of course, when the espadrille was on the other foot they were allowed to sleep with whichever *ingénue* was close at hand.

She was soft then. She was young and open and excited and naive.

But they hardened her, these men with their questions and their snide reviews. Their prodding and probing. Cajoling. They all tried to sleep with her and they all turned bitter when she rebuked them. Every single one of them. The other musicians, the soundmen, the roadies. The label guys.

As was well documented at the time, it was a fist and a cracked tooth at a residential studio somewhere in deepest Cornwall that brought about the dissolution of one of the most successful male-female duos of the era. This was the early eighties and by then she had grown a tough hide to protect herself. It felt like the world had grown hard too.

She drove straight back to London on the B-roads that night and never sang with Simon Healy again. She couldn't write for years afterwards because there are no more love songs to be written when all you feel is hate – and her hatred struggled to find a melody to sustain it.

Soon enough – perhaps inevitably – the journalists came knocking after the initial press release had been issued to the weeklies. More men with more questions. She ignored them all and they wrote what they wanted anyway: that she was the bitch who broke Healy's heart; that the sensitive and fragile songwriter-of-a-generation had been left licking his wounds with only a guitar for company.

In the months that followed she saw history slowly being revised before her very eyes. Suddenly *their* songs were *his* songs. *Their* stories *his* stories. The new folk network and the industry types all took his side and in time her songs – songs written by her or *for* her – were being sung by younger, prettier versions of herself, stripped of all meaning on the lips of doe-eyed careerists.

He dined on heartache for the next decade, did Simon. He experimented with synthesisers. He got three studio albums out of their split.

She left him to it, left them all to it, remained tight-lipped. She retreated into children, divorce and domesticity. She slept around. She enjoyed the company of uncomplicated women. She lived. Breathed. Repaired.

———

'Do you have plans for the next album?'

'There won't be a next album.'

'No?'

'No.'

'But aren't you still under contract? I thought I read something about a covers collection.'

'Yes, believe it or not I still owe two more albums. I signed a six-album solo deal and have not exactly been what you would call productive. But another album? No. That's never happening.'

'How can you be sure?'

'Oh, I can be very sure,' she says.

'Never say never.'

'I just did.'

The writer pauses. Steels himself. Tries to be as casual as possible.

'And are you still in touch with Simon?'

He notices one eyelid flutter as he asks this. Her smile spreads. He can see her molars. He thinks of the time he badly sliced his hand on the jagged edge of a baked beans tin lid last winter. A bachelor's injury. He remembers the way the wound opened up and paused for a moment before the brilliant blood streamed out of it. That is what her smile reminds him of: a wound awaiting blood.

She rolls her eyes. She picks up her cup and looks away.

'Of course. We have a child.'

'What is he working on?'

She takes a sip. Shrugs. Says nothing.

'His last album – '

She cuts him off: 'I never heard it.'

'Does listening to the albums you made together bring back bad memories?'

She suppresses a sigh as best as she can.

'Everything from then brings back bad memories.'

The writer laughs but then sees that she is not joking.

'It must be strange being asked about him thirty years after your divorce?'

'Yet still you do.'

They fall silent. He clears his throat.

'What is your day-to-day life like?'

'Ordinary,' she says. 'Routine. Are people even interested in that?'

'Of course they are.'

'You think?'

'Yes. Aren't you?'

'What – interested in your day-to-day life? No. Not at all.'

The writer smiles.

'Are you always this guarded in interviews?'

'Yes,' she says. 'At least it says so on my Wikipedia page.'

'So you google yourself, then?'

'Well, yes. Sometimes, obviously.'

'What's the biggest myth you've read about yourself online?'

'That I can sing. And that I slept with Sting.'

'That you can sing?'

'Yes.'

'But you can.'

'I don't think so.'

'Of course you can. You're – '

'I know who I am. But I have little confidence in my abilities. Never have. Hence the guardedness.'

'Even after all these years?'

'Even after all these centuries.'

There is a pause.

'You've not asked about Sting.'

'I don't believe you'd lower yourself to sleep with him.'

'That's the right response.'

'So did you?'

'None of your business.'

She smiles. This time it is real. This time it is less like a wound and more like curtains opening on a summer's morning.

'Are you always this probing?'

'You think I'm probing?'

She shrugs.

'By all means tell me if you think any of my questions are out of line.'

She waves her hand. 'Oh, I don't care. You can ask me anything.'

'Anything?'

'Yes.'

'Are you hungry?'

'Am I hungry? Suddenly it's open season and that's your question?'

'Yes. Or, specifically, would you like to go out for some food?'

'We're already in a place that sells food. We're already out.'

'But would you like to go somewhere else that sells other types of food?'

'But why?'

Her eyes sparkle as she says this. The writer sees something in there. Hope, maybe. Or mischief. Longing, even.

'Because – '

He pauses. She comes to his salvation.

'Is the interview finished, then?'

'I don't know. Do you want it to be?'

'You remind me of my therapist,' she says.

'You're seeing a therapist?'

'Isn't everybody?'

'I'm not,' says the writer, and more quietly: 'But only because I can't afford one.'

'I can give you his number if you like. Anyway, I feel like I'm just getting warmed up. We can talk some more. Tell me about this other place that does food.'

A beat passes. The writer feels flustered.

'I don't know,' he says. 'I hadn't got that far.'

'You were being spontaneous.'

'Yes. I suppose I was.'

'But not that spontaneous. Your mouth wrote a cheque that your arse can't cash, as they say.'

Their coffee cups are empty. The writer watches as the wheels on his tape recorder turn. He is the only music journalist he knows who still uses one. Recently, the guitarist of a young band tipped for big things pointed at the machine and asked him, in all innocence, what it was, and then, when the writer told him, responded in a sort of affected stoned drawl that nevertheless did not disguise his good schooling: 'Wow, you must be really old.' Their debut album went Top 10 the following week. It sickens him to think that those little scrotes will soon be millionaires.

He pulls his mind back into focus.

'Well, then.'

This is his fallback phrase. A conversational comma.

'Well, then,' says the folk song singer, in a convincing act of mimicry.

'Thanks for your time. It's been really good talking to you.'

'You liar.' She smiles then says: 'So the interview is finished, then?'

'Yes. I suppose it must be.'

'You've got enough for your article or whatever it is?'

'I think so.'

'So we're officially no longer working now.'

As she says this she uses her fingers to put speech marks around the word *working*.

'Yes.'

'Good. Then we can go somewhere and eat food and not have to worry about talking with our mouths full. Everyone knows that interviews start once they're no longer "interviews".'

———

Barons Court is not Stockwell. The writer does not know the area so the folk song singer leads them to a neighbourhood restaurant. It is Turkish.

He is relieved when she says she needs to smoke a cigarette outside first. He smiles and offers her one of his but she shakes her head and takes out a menthol from a pocket hidden beneath her scarves.

'We're a dying breed,' he says, but she doesn't laugh.

The humidity is cloying. The air feels close and dense and the sky is a tumult of clouds folding in on themselves. Shades of pale purple and sepia streak across it. The writer thinks he can hear a distant rumble, though it could be traffic coming off the Hammersmith Flyover nearby.

She holds her cigarette between her second and third fingers. Like Michel Houellebecq, he thinks. He wonders whether it is an affectation that has stuck or a practical necessity. She pecks at the cigarette like a bird unearthing a half-submerged worm after a rainfall.

They smoke in silence for a minute and then she looks at her cigarette and says, 'I'm down to three a day. Doctor's orders, though it makes no difference now.'

'Me too,' he says. 'Three lighters.'

For a moment she looks at him, confused, and then realising that it is a quip she smiles briefly before pushing her cigarette into the sand-filled ashtray. The butt stands there, bent and dirty like the burned stump of a bonsai. His is still only half-smoked.

'Have you always lived around here?' he asks.

'No, of course not,' she says, and then turning adds, 'Come on, then' and enters the restaurant.

Seated, she orders grilled salmon and he has kleftiko lamb. No starters. They both have wine. She white, he red. They eat awkwardly, no longer sure of their roles or what they are doing here.

He asks, 'Have you ever considered writing your memoirs?'

'No,' she replies.

'Really – never?'

'Plenty of people have mentioned it to me but I've never considered it, no.'

'Why?'

The folk song singer slowly breaks apart her salmon with a fork. She eats a small amount of bulgar wheat salad. He wishes he had ordered something less messy.

'Why? Because it would be a boring read.'

The writer picks up a piece of lamb and runs a fork down the bone of it. Feathers of meat fall away.

'I find that hard to believe. You've seen the world, met so many other famous musicians. Sung on all those sessions. You've achieved so much. I'm sure you have a lot of stories that readers would be interested in and plenty of dirt to dish. I know a publisher or two who would be desperate to get their hands on it.'

'Dishing dirt is precisely *not* what I want to do,' she says. 'Anyway, lots of people have seen the world and lots of people have achieved things of far greater significance. What if it didn't sell?'

'Would that matter?'

'Yes, of course. Knowing that only a couple of hundred people thought that your life was of interest would be crushing, don't you think?'

'It would still be a couple of hundred more than if I published my memoirs.'

'The shops are full of unread books,' she says.

She moves flakes of salmon around her plate then continues.

'Well, anyway. I'm not a writer. I'm not suggesting that you, as a journalist, record an album of pastoral ballads or wassailing songs so I don't see why I should presume to master your chosen art form, if you can call it that.'

'You could get a ghostwriter. A collaborator.'

'Are you fishing for work here?'

'No. I'm really not. Not at all. I hadn't thought about it until just now.'

'Good.' She points her fork at his plate. 'How is the lamb?'

'Nice. Very tender.'

The folk song singer abandons her food. She puts down her cutlery and instead picks up her wine, drains her glass and then signals the waiter for more.

'Have you written any biographies?'

'No,' says the writer. 'Not yet. I'm working on a couple of novels, though.'

'It is my experience that every music journalist is working on a couple of novels.'

'Probably. That's probably true.'

'Are you interested in writing biographies?'

'Are you fishing for a biographer here?'

'No,' says the folk song singer. 'But I might need someone to write an accurate obituary.'

———

The restaurant feels airless. The folk song singer can feel it pressing against her. Encasing her, almost.

They have finished eating. The writer's plate is empty, hers has barely been touched.

She removes her scarves and for a moment the writer looks at her neck – at the throat that has produced so much music – and then he sips more wine.

'We should have bought bottles instead of glasses,' she says. 'More economical.'

There is a rumble of thunder outside, sonorous and foreboding. She flinches. It sounds unreal, like a studio effect.

'A storm,' he says.

'We'll have to drink our way through it,' she says, then excuses herself.

In the bathroom she puts down the toilet lid and sits on it. She holds her stomach and takes tiny breaths. It is even warmer in here. Close. The air is a piece of elastic that has been pulled to snapping point. It has an energy to it, a potential.

She is bent double clutching her stomach. Her head is between her knees. She tries to control the pain in the way she was taught, through controlled breathing and mental projection. Meditation for beginners. It does not seem to work and she stays like this for a long time.

When she straightens and stands, the pain has finally decreased.

From her pocket she pulls a sheet of tablets and pops two of them out. She swallows them dry. Sees herself in the mirror. Leaves.

––––––

She is old if sixty is considered old, though it is difficult to tell any more.

He knows where and when she was born and the names of her parents. What school she went to. Star sign.

He is thirty-five. She does not know this. She does not know anything about him. He thinks that thirty-five is no longer considered young. He is not sure. Everything seems so mixed up. His is the generation of arrested development. He knows people – husbands, fathers – whose hobbies are computer games and skateboards. Isn't he, with his vast collection of vinyl and his faddish fixations on certain films or songs and an inability to get what his mother once called a proper job, stuck in some sort of perpetual sub-student existence too?

Then again, this is London and no one grows up in London. They come here for many reasons. For escape, reinvention. To make it. But never to grow old gracefully.

And people meet in the middle these days too. This is what he tells himself: people meet in the middle. Twenty-year-olds can date forty-year-olds and forty-year-olds sixty-year-olds. It is no big thing. Loneliness does not age-discriminate.

'You need to tell me something about yourself.'

She says this as the waiter hovers with a dessert menu for a moment before she waves him away. Though she does not intend it to, this statement comes out as an accusation.

'Why?'

'To redress the balance. It's only fair.'

The edges of their words are blurred now. They are both flushed from the wine, flushed from the humidity of the stifled night and the understanding that the storm is veering towards their clammy corner of the city. A strand of the folk song singer's hair is stuck to her forehead. The writer has loosened his shirt. There is perspiration on his upper lip.

'OK, then. When I was seven years old I saw a man die.'

'Fantastic. So what happened?'

'We were on a train. Me and my mother. I can't remember where we were going but a man stuck his head out of the window just before the train entered a tunnel.'

'Jesus. And then what happened?'

'Do you really want to know?'

'Well, you've started your little story now so yes. Yes, I do.'

'His head came off. People started screaming.'

'His head came *off*?'

'It was taken off, yes. By the force of the blow. But the funny thing was his body remained where it was.'

'And you saw this?'

'All I really remember is the noises that people around me made – sort of horrified groans; sounds I had never heard adults make before or since. And then the screech of the brakes being applied. The man was still standing there. I could see his fingers curled around the glass of the lowered window. He was wearing trainers. There was a carrier bag by his feet. It was full of hats.'

The folk song singer looks at him, aghast.

'All sorts of hats,' says the writer.

'And then what happened?'

'The train was delayed for ages. I suppose they were trying to find his head.'

She looks at him for a moment and then she bursts out laughing. She laughs for a long time.

She laughs until she is sobbing.

———

When they have drunk enough wine for their hips to bump together as they leave the restaurant she says to him 'How big is it?' and when he looks at her she says 'I mean how long is it, the piece?' and he laughs and says 'I don't even know, maybe two or three pages, my editor said I should see how it goes' and the folk song singer says 'And how has it gone?' and the writer says 'Good, it has gone really well' and then they find themselves standing in the road and the sky cracks again and it is nearly dark now as a taxi swishes past and they both ignore it and a flash of lightning makes her eyes look even bluer than they are and it makes the puddles blue too and then it starts raining.

It starts raining hard and she grabs his elbow and they begin to run as the rain seems to shift up a gear. The sound of it is all they can hear.

———

She is used to better men than him. But it has been a long time.

He is two years younger than her son, and in a strange way that is exciting, but in another more obvious way it is depressing. She tries not to think about it.

In her flat he feels like an invasion. In her private space he seems to her to have doubled in size.

'Do you live here alone?' he asks.

'Sometimes,' she says.

'I like it,' he says. 'Good light.'

She is barefoot and drunker than she has been in several years as she opens the sash window and lets London in.

It has stopped raining and now the room smells fertile. Gamey. When she turns around she expects to see steam rising from the writer but instead he is crouched down looking at her bookcase.

She opens more wine but it has not been chilled and it is hard to drink, so in the absence of anything else to do she fills the silence and the awkward space between them by leading the writer through to her bedroom.

When he lays her down and kisses her flesh he thinks of Anne Bancroft in *The Graduate* and the phrase *cookie dough* and how when her cells were first joining together rationing still existed and Elvis had not yet entered Sun Studio. He thinks: This is the body that sang 'We Walk Through the Woodlands'. He thinks: This body is responsible for magic. It is a legendary body.

Many people have written about the person inside it. They have paid money to see the owner of this body and they have dreamed about that person when sleeping. And now, he thinks, I am kissing the skin that holds it together. I am writing my own biography with my lips. I am tasting history.

As he presses her against the mattress and his mouth finds its way to hers she does not think about her new album or her career or music or Dustin Hoffman in *The Graduate* or the body of the stranger who is shifting and breathing on top of her. Instead she thinks about all the paperwork that she has yet to sort out, all the loose ends to tie up, all the arrangements yet to make, the painful conversations that she will have to have. She thinks about solicitors and accountants and doctors, an army of doctors, and how everyone remembers the first time but do they remember the last time?

She thinks about how exits are inherently complicated when they should be simple, and how a full stop can only truly be used once in a life.

The Museum of Extinct Animals

The Museum of Extinct Animals is many things. It is a labyrinth of dusty secrets. It is a fortress of fallen totems from another time. It is a symposium of ghosts.

The Museum of Extinct Animals is a cathedral-sized capsule containing stuffed creatures of rare distinction.

A macabre zoo of man's making. A cemetery of memory.

Here they are corralled and curated. They sit on shelves or in cabinets, stuffed and stitched, framed and mounted, perfectly pinned.

These are creatures in perpetual stasis, immortalised in repose, never to stalk the meadows, swim the deepest briny oceans or fly across great fields of blood-red poppies in spring again.

The Museum of Extinct Animals is a maudlin place. Dust gathers in knee-deep drifts and thousands of dead flies and moths litter the surfaces of the glass cases as if they too are clamouring to be part of this grotesque menagerie. The silence is so deep and sorrowful it sounds like a gassed orchestra and the only light is that which finds a way through the tiniest gap in the old blinds that have been left unopened for decades.

The building houses a collection of the world's hunted, neglected, fetishised, collected, colonised, coveted, repressed, dissected. The tortured and the eaten. It is a monument to human greed and stupidity. A vulgar cenotaph to ignorance.

No one ever enters the Museum of Extinct Animals, except for the caretaker. He is too afraid to tell anyone about it in case the last remaining samples of once-glorious animals are stolen or destroyed. He lives in constant fear.

Little is known of the caretaker, other than that he is very old and has never married. Some believe him to be Austrian, though this has never been confirmed. He is paid a small monthly stipend for his minimal duties by an organisation discreetly registered to an address in France, which when visited proved to be a charcuterie in a small Alpine village. Its owner claimed to know nothing about the museum or the caretaker and appeared more concerned with a late delivery of duck rillettes.

To explore the Museum of Extinct Animals is to undertake time travel. To enter it is to step into an alternative earth, a living map of different countries and eras and regions and climate changes and hunting patterns and food chains and urban growth and rainforest destruction and centuries of regress, all collated into one three-dimensional monument to misfortune.

The creatures are weird and wonderful, ugly and beautiful. Looking at them evokes first a fear of the unknown, as many of these species are unrecognisable, some having not been seen alive by human eyes for hundreds of years. Then comes a crushing sense of melancholy that follows the realisation that time only ever moves forward, and that you can never reverse death. It is just not possible.

But it is not time that has slain these creatures, it is man, and for that perhaps it is *he* who should be gathering dust on a shelf in a pose that best represents his species: poised, perhaps, with a rifle tucked under one arm and the other hand shading his brow as he squints off into the distance with a hint of bloodlust in his eyes. That is the human stance. The killer's posture.

In many ways the Museum of Extinct Animals is an inverse graveyard. The corpses have been unearthed from the soil of the past and exhibited, each with a name tag and a plaque bearing a date of final extinction. Some of the great losses are alarmingly recent, like that of the Pyrenean ibex, a wild horned mountain goat (rendered extinct on 6 January 2000, Spain). This suggests that the collection is continually being added to, though no one knows when or by whom because the Museum of Extinct Animals mainly exists in academic papers and rumours, in urban mythology and internet forums, in the imaginations of those who fall asleep at night dreaming of great plains and savannah clearings inhabited by all the species that ever lived.

There are those who might even be able to remember what it was they were doing the very day that the last Pyrenean ibex's little heart stopped beating. Could anyone have done anything to help anyway? It's difficult to say.

Elsewhere in the museum there sit creatures whose extinctions stretch back through less ecologically enlightened times. Creatures such as the great auk (3 June 1844, Iceland), an animal superficially similar to the penguin, 'an excellent swimmer' whose wings doubled up as fins underwater but who, unlike other auks, could not fly, which made it more vulnerable to humans and other predators.

According to the small engraved description exhibited in the Museum of Extinct Animals, 'the great auk laid only one egg each year and was hunted for food and down for mattresses'.

So perhaps even now someone, somewhere, is sleeping atop extinction each night.

Or what of the aurochs (Poland, 1627), whose name translates as 'primeval ox', or 'proto-ox', and of whom no photographs exist, only cave paintings, for the horned aurochs was an animal worshipped by humans and sacrificed to the gods accordingly. The mammal survived the Iron Age, changing weather systems and threatened food supplies and indeed flourished across Europe, but what it did not survive was continual encounters with *humans*.

The aurochs population dwindled and its movements became restricted to Poland, Lithuania and parts of Prussia. In 1564, according to a royal survey, Polish gamekeepers knew of only thirty-eight such animals. The last recorded aurochs was a female who, without a male with which to procreate, lost her entire reason to exist and curled up and died amongst the dead leaves and the comforting wet smell of woodland fecundity and decay. Location: Jaktorów Forest. Date: 1627. Exact day unknown. The laws of probability suggest it was a weekday.

Perhaps you are now beginning to understand that the Museum of Extinct Animals is no showpiece, no tawdry end-of-the-pier cheap thrill. No. It is a giant filing cabinet of human error. It is simply too sad a place to enter without due preparation.

Of course, were visitors ever to wander its vast and sorrowful galleries, after a short time of reflection most would straighten up, dab at their eyes and become indignant, saying, 'It's nothing to do with me', and then go about their business as if extinction itself were extinct.

What is equally difficult to reconcile is why someone would go to the trouble of recording the execution of the last remaining animal of a specific species – the aforementioned great auk, 3 June 1844, for example – but not actually stop and do something about its preservation. When sailors speared that last auk on the island of

Eldey, ten miles off the south-west coast of Iceland, they carefully documented the minutiae of its demise. To do so they may have had to remove their fur-lined mittens in order to dig out a piece of paper and a gnarled stub of a pencil in those sub-zero, frostbitten conditions.

But that's as far as their commitment went. After all, you sleep much better on a down mattress than on a bed made from a glacier.

The exhibits are arranged by species and continent. The North American Fish section alone is nothing short of a roll-call of senseless slaughter and greedy plunder, once-poetic names now nothing more than dried-out relics: the Snake River sucker (Wyoming, 1928), the Alvord cutthroat (Nevada and Oregon, 1940), the Pahrump Ranch killifish (Nevada, 1958), the thick-tail chub (California, 1957), the blackfin cisco (Great Lakes, 1960s), the longjaw cisco (Great Lakes, 1970s).

Beyond that is the vast section that houses the mammals, then a short airless corridor leads into the cavernous hall in which the hundreds of extinct birds are mounted and framed. The ceiling in this room is so high that it appears one inch square when viewed from below.

Naturally the room of ex-birds features perhaps the most famously non-existent creature of them all, the doomed breed made famous by Lewis Carroll and visualised by schoolchildren everywhere when they hear the word *extinction*: the dodo (Mauritius, 1693).

The corridors seem endless. Rooms lead to other rooms. Drifts of dust gather. The silence is external, a vortex of auditory nothingness into which the occasional shaft of light permeates to illuminate a small plaque screwed into the wall:

Reptiles, Asia, 1820–1840.

One unavoidable question arises, one you might already have asked yourself: Why does the Museum of Extinct Animals even exist?

The answer is simple: it exists for the same reason anything exists. Because it does.

For now it is safe, as so few know about it, yet even the museum is not impervious to threat. Once its precise whereabouts and purpose are made public, humans will in time destroy it too, and then someone will have to open up a Museum of Extinct Museums.

And then that too, of course, will be vulnerable to elimination.

And so the cycle goes.

POSTSCRIPT TO 'THE MUSEUM OF EXTINCT ANIMALS'

January 2002. The research party had been wandering the forests, swamps and bayous of Louisiana Pearl River Wildlife Management Area for many days. They had been camping under the stars and eating frugally. No one complained about the humidity and the mosquito bites, nor the rashes, for they had come equipped with nets and an arsenal of sprays, creams and repellents. Modern-day explorers and conservationists don't have to suffer like their forefathers did, and that's one thing they could thank the chemical industry for.

There was a shared common goal to the expedition, something of far greater importance than a few itchy bites and a good eight hours' sleep: sighting the ivory-billed woodpecker.

This strange and mysterious creature had been declared an endangered species on 11 March 1967, after hundreds of years of logging and hunting had destroyed its habitats and drastically reduced breeding numbers.

It had been officially declared extinct in 1994, though there were some who disputed this. There were just enough vocal voices of dissent to instil hope for the birdwatchers, conservationists, academics and students who had a vested interest – whether scientific, ornithological or emotional – in the ivory-billed woodpecker.

Unconfirmed sightings had been on the increase when the party entered the bayou armed with maps and binoculars, camouflage and oh-so-silent cameras, plus all the sundry items needed to survive comfortably on an expedition into these unforgiving, barely penetrable wetlands of the South.

The first week or so passed without a sighting. There was much to see and do, so many creatures of many varieties to observe and a few million mosquitoes to evade, but the ivory-billed woodpecker remained something their minds had only ever imagined; a vision of a brilliant bird, elevated now to near-mythical status.

Then on the tenth day came the familiar 'double-knock' noise of a beak on bark, a sound familiar to the expedition party members only from recordings. It travelled through the heavy, wet air: *thock thock thock. . .*

No one moved.

They heard it again: *thock thock thock. . .*

Could it be. . . No? Surely not. They dared not utter its name.

As nervous fingers reached for sound recorder buttons, a dozen pairs of eyes scanned the dense swampland, the fetid mangroves and the shifting shades where the undergrowth met the water. All they saw was a tangle, a tussle between life and death, a never-ending war of species on species. Nature operating at maximum productivity.

And in amongst it all, its creator hidden from the well-trained eyes of the research party, the *thock thock thock* of its industry rising up from the past.

Was it? Yes, it was. Whisper the words: the ivory-billed woodpecker. It was alive, praise be, *alive*.

That simple sound of beak and bark was the sound of hope. Suddenly all was not lost. Man's cruel cycle of death had been defeated; the odds had been smashed.

The ivory-billed woodpecker, this late lamented creature, was back and in fine health: proud, glorious, free – and oblivious to its near miss as a late entrant into the Museum of Extinct Animals, about which the party members had attended seminars and read long, academic essays, yet of whose existence they had no clear evidence.

Or at least, confided the party and their two academic leaders, we *think* it's the sound of the ivory-billed woodpecker.

It certainly sounded like Old IB, as they had taken to calling it. But they had been up the river and into the swamps for some days now, and the isolated and ever-shifting environment had a strange effect on people. Could anyone see it? No. No, they could not.

Was it even the right call?

With blanket silence on the bird front once again, now the seeds of hope grew into shoots of doubt. Perhaps, suggested one student, it was distant gunfire. After all, the area was rife with hunters and trappers, and hadn't they run into that party of men yesterday who everyone had made *Deliverance* jokes about as soon as they were out of earshot?

A couple of the other students offered murmurs of agreement: yes, it could be those crazy hunters firing their old-time Civil War guns, their echoes returning like lost postcards from the past.

Quick, they decided. Split up into groups. Get organised. Search the undergrowth, explore the trees, scour the groves. The old spread-and-circle routine. There's no time to lose. Let's undertake a clockwise sweep, they said.

The entire expedition felt galvanised into action, all of them certain they should be doing something in the search for the *thock thock thock* of the ivory-billed woodpecker.

They found nothing. The sighting was recorded as unconfirmed because it wasn't even a sighting. It was a noise, a suggestion of Old IB, a symbol of a creature that no longer exists.

Maybe *thock thock thock* was a ghost of the last-known ivory-billed woodpecker, forever trapped in the hinterlands of the bayou, wandering the dark corridors of Louisiana, its ghost beak pecking ghost trees and destined to drive men mad for generations to come.

POST-POSTSCRIPT TO 'THE MUSEUM OF EXTINCT ANIMALS'

Monroe County, Arkansas, 11 February 2004. Over 697 million cameras in the world and only one of them captures an ivory-billed woodpecker in flight – or the ghost of one at the very least, for who can tell the difference anyway?

First one, then another, then another. Seven sightings over the next fourteen months of ghost birds or otherwise, each with a distinctive blood-red plumage.

POST-POST-POSTSCRIPT TO 'THE MUSEUM OF EXTINCT ANIMALS'

'I have heard the summer dust crying to be born.'
—Robinson Jeffers

An English Ending

At six it was a black mirror capturing and framing the first settled shapes of the rising sun, but by seven the reservoir held ten thousand triangles of light that reconfigured themselves across the surface like a shoal of rising herring.

There was a light breeze too, and birdsong from the curlews and house martins as they rode the unseen currents of air. They were joined by a scattering of late-arriving swallows who settled to dip their beaks and ruffle their feathers after their long journey across the Sahara and up through Morocco, Spain, France and the length of England. Their flight was nearly complete. In the surrounding dells and copses they would make their nests, replenish their energy levels and breed. They would rest for three months until summer's end, then take flight once more before the winter's frost tightened across the skin of the north once again.

The woman was out of breath when she reached the crest of the hill as it flattened out on to the open vastness of the moor. She felt a cold crescent of sweat across her lower back. Damp, her blouse clung to her flesh.

She turned to take in the view of the town down below, snaking its way along the narrow valley's floor, and surrounding it the scattering of hamlets and houses that worked their way up the opposite hillside, their mullion windows and stout lintels suggesting a permanence at odds with the changing landscape that grew around them. Closer by she saw seasonal whin, moorland moss and the wild grasses that sounded like shale and pebbles shifting in the shallows of a shore when the wind shook their tussocks. Beyond them, reaching off into the distance, the slow-turning blades of the turbines and the strung cables linking pylons that stretched ominously like automatons; they always made her think of the Ted Hughes story they'd read at school that told of a giant metal man careering through the landscape.

This was her valley; it was all she had known or might ever know. For the first time, this realisation that the valley represented the limit of her life struck her as a concrete fact rather than circumstantial supposition.

———

The reservoir had been sunk by labourers armed with winches and ropes and pickaxes a hundred years ago or more. She had read about it. There had been a book about its origins in the local library, one of the few places where she felt she could lose herself for several hours.

They were Irishmen, mainly. Two thousand of them at one point, living in prefabricated huts up here at the top of the world, in a makeshift township in which there was also a store and a recreation room. Alcohol, the book had reported, was strictly prohibited on the site, so to drink the men had to take the walk down into the town – the same hike she had just done in reverse. Only the most committed alcoholics would do that after a twelve-hour shift breaking rocks tipped from mine carts at ten-minute intervals.

The woman walked to the water's edge. She shivered at the sight of it, though not from the cold. It was the hostility of this place that had always excited her. It scared her too, and this fear and excitement combined to evince a strange sensation within. A curious sense of awe, perhaps.

Even now, after a lifetime of visiting it, the portentous power of the black water was magnetic. She was drawn to it, continually. She returned again and again, whenever the noise in her head reached deafening levels or her body felt the pull of gravity too strongly, stomping up the hill in winter to watch snowflakes settle on the icy skin that formed on its shallow corners, then picking her way back down in evening darkness. The lights of the town below her only guide.

Her husband had long since stopped accompanying her. Once, they had been young and in love, and their future had been a bright ball of fire as certain as the burning sun, and they had climbed the hill with a blanket and a basket and made a day of it, stepping hand in hand, like generations of couples before them. Then they had stripped and swum and dried off on the rocks that lined the giant basin; rocks chiselled and shaped by the rough callused hands of rough callous men born into a century already alien today.

As the water lapped at shoes inappropriate for the terrain, she stooped and washed the stains from her hands. She watched the dark-brown patches come alive again and then drip from her skin, one red droplet at a time, diluting into nothingness, two dozen drops amongst fifty thousand square metres of water.

She kicked off her pumps and slowly began to remove her clothes. She saw the flecks and droplets on her blouse. The dried dots as mute reminders. She felt too the throbbing in her knuckles and wrists. She touched the jagged, crusted graze on her neck that looked like a Morse code message scratched into her skin, and inspected the fading marks left by digits that had curled too tightly around forearms and loose biceps.

As she folded her garments she tried not to look at a body she barely recognised. She felt her way around folds and ripples that she did not remember, but which mapped a body near ruined by childbirth. His words, not hers: Birthing has ruined you. Ruined *it*.

There had been no turning moment – no single deciding factor – but rather a series of barbed comments, laden silences and the occasional burst of noise or movement that had seemed too large and complicated for their restricted domestic life. The collapse of what once was had been comprised of dozens of gestures, scores of things left unsaid and hundreds of resentments spread over the thousands of days that all stacked up to create millions of tiny moments of muffled misery. Drink had played its part too – him, not her – though it had only brought out what was already there: a nasty streak that had spread within him like rust. This bitterness had become a parasite that strangled any compassion she still believed he must once have had.

She had watched the steady souring of this man she'd mistakenly thrown her lot in with.

She had swum here as a child. She had played and paddled and splashed here. Warm sticky pop and wasps and crisps you could wear on your fingers like rings. Dragonflies scudding low across the water. T-shirt suntans. Insect bites. The evaporating vapour trails of distant planes.

The water bit as she walked into it. Snapped at her. She felt the shock of it in the tiny bones in her feet and then in her ankles and running up through her legs.

She had not slept and she needed this jolt.

Only as the reservoir took her breath away did she realise that this was why she had left the house with its curtains closed and the duvet balled and tangled and stained and clotted, a chair upended and the kitchen drawer hanging open, to walk through town just as the sky was streaking with the first tendrils of morning, then on up the hill to step silently into this vast black body of water: because she had needed to feel the cold water quicken her pulse. To move beyond intuition or instinct and instead experience the visceral.

She disturbed the perfect stillness and let herself fall forward, half diving and half flopping into it. They say that the submerging of the heart is the hardest part. Once that has felt the shock of the cold, then the rest of the body follows. The blood pumps, the skin stiffens and dimples.

She put her heart beneath the meniscus and held it there, then went all the way under. Her senses rushed to readjust.

When she emerged, the woman pulled herself forward with a breaststroke. As a teenager she had been a strong swimmer. Athletic, even. She had had a body suited to it and a northern constitution untroubled by the challenging elements. She was not one of those who broke the ice in winter to prove something to others, yet she could always withstand a level of coldness that others had withdrawn from. She could withstand many more things then, but time and circumstance had chipped away at her resistance until she felt she could no longer breathe and something snapped.

The computer. That was to blame too, along with many other things. The amount of time he spent on it, pretending to be working on his 'project', an amorphous pursuit whose content and purpose had changed over the years. First it was documenting the birdlife of the upland way, and then it was researching a book about the history of all the old mills in the area, then building a website about myths and legends of the valley. Then something about real ale – perhaps.

But she knew the truth of it. The adult sites. The films and the photos and the chat rooms. Filth. She would rather he had gone off with someone else than pursue betrayal through quiet neglect. At least affairs were tangible. Actions that warranted reactions.

———

Her feet searched for the bottom of the reservoir but they could not find it, so she swam on, out towards the centre. Here, from the middle of this huge hollow on the hilltop, a new view presented itself. Beyond the boulders of the basin's rim there was nothing visible but water and sky, their colours combining and merging into one sweep of cloud and sunlight, and all around her those shimmering triangles that played upon the surface like shards of a mirror smashed in anger.

Blood. She felt it coursing around her body as if bubbles were fizzing through her arms and into her fingertips. She felt effervescent, drunk on her own internal fire.

She thought of the children for the first time since those early hours when the night had slowed and swirled and the house had seemed like an endless new dimension of darkening horror. For a moment she regretted their existence, if only for the repercussions they would have to suffer. Not just the trauma of their losses but also the burden of history. The stigma of a family name from this day forward.

The woman turned on to her back and saw the shore far off in the distance. She could just make out her shoes neatly placed side by side. The water felt smooth and viscous against her skin, like oil. Like mercury.

And it wasn't just the drink or the computer or the moods. Unemployment also. Her having to work and cook and shop and clean while he devoted himself to inertia and cruelty. And he *had* been cruel – and very good at it too. *Manipulative* was the word she would use. That ability to twist and control. To wear masks. To deceive.

There were many things she wished she had said over the years. All those retorts that only ever came later, when her anger had simmered. But instead she had held them inside her. Made herself into a bottle and kept the resentments there, locked away. But bottles pop and bottles break. The pressure builds or something cracks.

She swam for a long time. She swam with her eyes closed and felt the morning unfurl around her. She felt the full, rising sun on her face and heard the birdsong again. The woman swam until her legs and arms ached and a hunger grew in her stomach like an opening bud.

In the end, it had been the tiniest thing. A trigger. Certainly nothing that she could have predicted. Not a raised hand but a sneer – the same sneer she had seen a thousand times but would never see again: one of disbelief at the announcement of her avowed intention to educate herself. To better herself. To move her life onwards, beyond him.

She had rehearsed her announcement for weeks, only for it to be met with a sneer and one word, repeated: You? *You?*

A sneer and that one word, and then an object being thrown. Her hand grasping at something. The picture frame, was it? No. It had felt heavier in her hand than that. She couldn't for the life of her remember what, though. Something that could do damage. And then the fight back. Fists and knuckles and nails. A grappling. Fingers at her throat. A cracked mirror. The kitchen drawer. A frantic hand feeling for something. The cat fleeing. And all the while silence, save only for the sound of their own heavy, awkward breathing and their feet squeaking on the lino. No words. Just a thrusting and then an alien sensation of metal and flesh. Metal into flesh. A final release of pressure, years of it, released like a burst tyre. A puncture. Messy, yet contained. An English ending.

And then the stains drying in the rising morning sun.

She was as far from land as she could get now. The reservoir surrounded her and she could swim no more. She slowly trod water and kicked her legs just enough to keep her mouth above the surface. Exhaustion pulled at every muscle, then turned her limbs to stone.

In the far distance she saw the wild moorland grasses bending with the breeze. The water felt colder here. Cold and dark and deep. Perhaps, she thought, the reservoir was not a reservoir at all, but the great, gaping opening of a tunnel that ran for miles into the centre of the earth.

A tiny feather floated beside her. It was down from a duck or a goose, curled upwards in such a way that it looked sculptural as it lay upon the unbroken surface, only a small part of it actually touching the water. Perfectly buoyant.

The woman watched it float there, undisturbed, alone, brilliant, white, perhaps the last pure and beautiful thing left in the world.

A River

As a boy he tickled trout here. He learned to lift the sleepy fish slowly from the river as if they were sunken silver treasures, raising them like gleaming offerings to the burning sun.

As a teenager he swam in cool bubbling pools the colour of over-stewed tea and later, as a young man, he returned to propose to his wife on the bankside as the winter water ran by like mercury and hip-flask whiskey warmed their throats.

Now he has three children and often when he drives along the motorway he remembers the river that flowed where today there is nothing but miles of bitumen, smiling with tears in his eyes as he recalls the way the light hit the fishes' scales, turning them into bejewelled objects of wonder.

The Longest, Brightest Day

The stalks of wheat part as the dogs run ahead into the golden thickness of the field, flushing out whatever creature might be crouched there, cowering in its shallow hollows.

The woman calls them back as the man steers the swine herd with a flick-crack of a split birch branch behind their ears. One hound returns, but the other has pushed on through the patch that stretches as far as the earth's undulations allow.

The woman whistles and the man shouts.

He grabs the first dog by a knot of skin at the back of its neck and twists it to stillness.

They see the other hound carve a darting path of flattened grain through the field, and then it stops and everything is still for a moment, and even the swine seem to pause in unison. The sun is beating down on them and they are slothful. They think only of the next shaded pool, the next drink.

The day hums with more unseen insects than there are stars in the night sky.

Then something explodes upwards from the wheat field: a fat bird taking clumsy flight. It is too far away for the man to bring down with spear or slingshot.

And then, a moment later, a hare comes tearing from the wheat and makes for the stubbled open meadow beyond it. The hare is only running at half-speed, the tensile sinews of its hind legs flexing, its nostrils flared and ears cocked to track the frantic steps of the dog that is far behind it, a diminishing dot slowing in the heat.

'Useless hound,' says the man, but he is already looking around for danger signs. He knows that a cultivated field means people, and people mean trouble, especially if their crop has been trampled upon by strangers driving beasts.

The woman whistles and this time the dog turns back. They wait for it, and when it comes to heel it is wide-eyed and panting, but they do not let it rest. The man gestures to the hill ahead of them with his split birch stick, and the woman understands.

They press on.

They find water and a place for the hogs to drink and to wade in the cool shadows of a leafy overhang.

The noise they make disturbs a heron, which unfolds its wings and rises flying from its nest. It banks towards the sun, a black shape set against the white glare of the long dry season, its beak stitching the sky with invisible thread.

The man unwraps a large rag containing nuts and acorns and he scatters them for the pigs, who greedily gulp them, and then he unrolls a stiff hide and they both rest a while.

When they wake the woman carefully reaches into her pouch and lifts three eggs from a loose basket of protective hawthorn branches.

At the edge of the trees she crouches and breaks the egg on a rock, then tips the contents on the dry earth. She takes something from her pocket. It is a small branch that she strips of its dried leaves, and these she crumbles and stirs with a stick into the mess while muttering words to herself.

The woman carefully taps around the crown of the second egg with a flint head until there is a hole and she gives it to the man, who speaks some unheard words to the ground, a private prayer or incantation, and then tips it back and swallows the contents. She does the same, wiping a gluey string from her chin.

A fistful of nuts and hard dried beans follow. They chew slowly and quietly, crunching them between the jagged surfaces of their worn teeth.

The dogs lie on their sides near the water, their chests rising and falling.

The stream is shallow. Many fish hang suspended in the current. They are each of a hand's length and they dart in different directions when the man bends over and tugs at a clump of cress, shaking the drops from it. He chews a leaf then he gives the woman some.

He swallows, and squints towards the sun.

'Far?' he wonders, but she just shrugs and begins to roll up the hide, then pulls the pouch cord over her head to rest on the narrow bone of her shoulder.

She whistles to the sleeping dogs and their indolent eyes turn in their heads, and then they slowly stand.

————

As they walk, the sun is a scowling face that snaps at their heels. The sun stings like nettles on their dirt-dark necks. The sun is the tiny creatures that crawl and fly and feast on flesh, gorging on the thick, wet redness that pulses within skin.

They lick their lips and their lips taste of river stones. They swallow and swallow again.

The dogs stop and sigh, their rough tongues unrolling like strips of tanned wrist lagging.

The sun is harvest-time blisters and skin stripped bare. The sun is the prickles of thorns plucked. The sun is a song that keeps singing. The sky is clear and still and it urges them to join the bones of their fathers.

————

They trudge onwards, following the swine that stray across the plain.

The dogs keep the herd from wandering away and the man and woman adjust the hides, the pouches, the food and the tools that are strapped across their backs.

They feel exposed out on the plain but know that anyone approaching them will be seen too.

The trees offer cover but it is also where people have made their homes in clearings made by rooting out stumps, felling trees, setting traps.

It has not rained for a long time and the green grass is turning yellow. Fissures split the soil and they pass several parched quags where once there was water but now there are only drooping rushes and thickets of wilting nettles.

As she walks, the woman idly rubs the heads of grass until they turn to dust and then she winds the grass stalks around her fingers. She ties them until they snap or unravel and fall to the ground. She pulls out more long, dry strands and plaits them into tight, neat strips and later she will tie them at eyeline on low branches to help guide the way back.

The woman has heard stories told of these wide-open quarters being used to grow new things to eat; more produce than a man or woman or family could ever need. She wonders what will await them across the bone-dry plains and if, when they reach that point where the sky meets the land, everything will drop away into a deep black pit of nothingness.

But the sky keeps going and the land keeps going.

Through daytime and darktime.

Going and going.

Endless.

———

He watches her. He looks at the back of her head. He admires the way she walks, the shape of her.

He remembers how her strong hips feel when he curls his hand around the bone there.

She is skilled and brave too. She can craft things and she has the knowledge of the land. Is useful with her hands. She can lift. Navigate. Forage. Manage the animals.

He feels excited when he sees tiny beads of sweat gather on her top lip, or when she smiles at him from a distance.

He enjoys watching her peel off her clothes to step into a pool, his eyes lingering on the dark target of the midriff, her brown skin turning golden. Her limbs becoming tangents when submerged.

The small dark dots on her back, her biceps.

———

The fields are the skin of the land.

Now and then the man and the woman discern the movement of shapes in the distance, and often they are aware of things in the grass, low scuttling creatures questing through the tangled wildness.

Up above, birds hover and screech, sometimes in great flocks in a perpetual state of reshaping, but at other times solitary species swoop down to snatch at something helpless, and lift it up and away to where the gods sit watching on.

'They say there is much water out there,' says the woman.

'I told you that,' comes the man's reply.

'No. I heard it before, in Father's stories. So much water, and so deep, that a man could never cross it.'

'The gods made it so.'

'I wonder why.'

'It is wasteful to wonder. Better to think about things that matter, like the swine, and what we will get for them.'

'They are good hogs.'

'Yes. Yes, they are.'

'We have reared them well.'

'Well enough.'

'At the circle in the centre of it all someone will want what we have to offer,' says the woman.

'I hope so,' says the man. 'We have been good to the gods, and the gods will be good to us.'

'I hope so too.'

'Hope is all we have.'
'And each other.'

———————

They enter the woods and stop and wait and listen. The packed trees flatten the day. Dark illusions are at play.

What sunlight penetrates here is shaped and trapped; is reduced to rectangles there on the ground.

They hear no voices, nor see any signs of life such as footmarks or scorched circles. They smell no latrines. The dogs instinctively corral the swine into a cluster and the man scratches behind their ears to reward them.

That night after they have found water, and they have all drunk from it until their trunks become swollen, he hog-ties the front legs of the swine with lengths of dried gut so that they must sit slumped forward, capable only of dragging their back legs, and when they do they scrape away the skin, and it hurts, so they don't. He feeds them the last of the nuts. They settle.

The man and woman are deep in the bracken, hidden from view. Here they press down a hide mattress then they lie on it close together in the thin, dry darkness, their arms around one another, their mouths open, breaths combining, and they dream of the sun and great stones and the huge waterfall of home until the birdsong is loud and the sun is stabbing at their eyes.

Only when the man goes to check on the swine does he see that one is missing.

He uses his hands to count again because he knows he has as many as he does fingers, but this time there are more fingers than swine.

He wades into the bracken, first in one direction and then the other. It has not been disturbed beyond the circle that has been flattened by them. It is unfathomable.

The man crouches down in the dirt to look for tracks, but the swine have scratched and swept the dust there so that it is impossible to see any other markings. Their scat is everywhere, strong. He studies the stalks and none seem snapped or bent.

The coolness of the early day is already slipping away, and his temples and back are wet with sweat.

The man wades further away into the bracken and the waxy fronds brush against his legs. The woman sees him and says, 'What?', but he doesn't reply as he circles the camp now, pushing through the plants and looking this way and that. He feels first panic and then fear, then anger, and then he arrives at resignation.

He returns to the swine and slowly begins to untie them. Each one stands up, stretches, and then begins to snuffle at the ground.

The woman is by his side. He points to them and in turn holds up his fingers. 'How?' says the woman, her eyes widening. 'Where?'

The man shrugs and shakes his head.

They both look beyond the ferns and into the trees and see that the sun is high, and they watch for a moment as beams of light play across the crisp carpet underfoot.

Here, beyond the towering columns of ancient tree trunks, unseen in the unknown beyond, a pod of birds noisily take flight.

———————

She uses the sun to guide them. They walk for a long time but they keep stopping to check the direction or to drink water, and to wash their faces and cool their feet, and to do the same for the beasts. They remove their rough garments and submerge them, then wear them wet. The dogs come alive in the water, and enjoy having it splashed in their faces. They try to bite gulps of it, as if it were a solid thing. The hogs trough and grunt and relish being scratched. They leave a trail of dung, though the man notices that the pellets are getting smaller, darker, drier and less frequent. He keeps thinking about the missing hog, and when he does he turns back and looks over his shoulder, and he sees the fields and hills rolling away behind them, and he sees the dotted knots of dense woodlands that link together to form throughways for the bears and the wolves and the deer and the foxes and the lynx and the polecats and all the other animals that stalk one another in the permanent death dance undertaken by all living things.

———————

The distant sky rumbles but there are no tumbling clouds or streaks of white or purple light, and the sky has not turned the copper colour of limestone water as it does on other such days that harbour storms.

They are in the grasslands and their clothes are covered in burrs, seeds and seed heads, and marked with smudges of pollen.

The man and woman look at each other, and the dogs stop, their pricked ears turning towards the source of the sound. Their tails go down, curling tight between their back legs. Though their view is obscured, they lower their bodies and fix their eyes towards the top edge of the fields. The rumbling gets louder and the man gestures with a hand for them to crouch. The sky signals no storm, yet it is wracked with the thud of something powerful, something larger than any living thing. A deep drumming.

Then suddenly shapes snap across the field line: black furious shifting shapes in a race across the path ahead. There is much jostling and there is the sound of snorting and breathing too, and hooves hammering at the hard loess as more horses than either of them can count go charging through the grasslands at the high end of the meadow. The two of them are close enough to see their manes as they bounce and thrash and their tails swing; close enough to feel the air around them become changed.

In amongst the herd are younger ponies running at full speed to keep up, their coats shining in the glare like minerals reflecting the sun. One or two falter in the grass beds but none fall.

Some of the horses trail strings of phlegm from mouths whose lips are peeled back to reveal big strong yellow teeth set like rocks in pink gums, and patches of white foam smear their rounded trunks.

They move as one.

Their twitching nostrils are wet and flared and their eyes are wide and black and wild as they search for something unseen, the target of their desires buried deep within the collective abandon of the wild charge, and the man and the woman grab on to the dogs, relieved that the horses are not running towards them, where they and their caravan would surely be trampled into the cracked earth.

The swine are disturbed but they cannot see the horses as they rumble off into the distance, a billowing cloud of dust and pollen and dandelion puffs the only sign of their passing. A deep silence settles across the plain.

The man and the woman smile, aware that they have witnessed wonder and beauty.

Tonight, in sleep, they hope to see the wild horses once again.

———

In the trees a tangle of vines block their trail once more.

They hang heavily weighted with great bunches of green grapes. Spherical, shining and succulent, the fruits are framed by fans of leaves and creeping stalks that wend their way around branch and limb.

The woman twists one off and sniffs it. She pops the skin and tastes the sweet spray of the juice, warm and sugary. The taste of the sun.

She chews through the flesh and before she has finished is already stuffing more into her mouth. One, two, three. The man does the same and soon they are crammed full and they are laughing through dripping lips. And then after they have each swallowed the grapes they kiss, their mouths meeting in a place beneath the branches.

They pull apart and she takes several grapes and crushes them underfoot. She says a prayer. She stirs them into the dirt. The skin and the flesh. The seeds. She mixes it all into the dry mud.

The man goes to feed the dogs some of the grapes too but she halts him by gripping his forearm.

'No,' she says. 'They're bad for dogs. Remember?'

Instead they feed the grapes to the pigs, who eat until they are belching and farting, and then the man and the woman carefully pick several more bunches and turn back from the impenetrable mass to pick a new way through the sunken maze of this island.

———

They walk through the trees for a long time and then they walk through the fields for an even longer time and sometimes they talk.

'What do you think is past these fields?' she asks.

'We have spoken of this already.'

'I know. But what do you think is past these fields?'

'Trees.'

'And what do you think is past the trees?'

He scratches at his beard before he speaks.

'More trees.'

'And after them?'

He hesitates. He thinks for a moment.

'More fields.'

Now it is her turn to hesitate.

'It can't just go on forever.'

'Why not?'

'Just fields and trees.'

'Yes. Yes, it can.'

'Just fields and trees forever.'

He nods.

'And big rocks and deep, dark rivers. And hills and plains. And the sky and the gods above and the gods below. And – '

'Yes?' She urges him on. She wants there to be more.

'And you know what else.'

For a moment she is puzzled. And then she remembers. Her face brightens.

'And the circle.'

'And the circle,' he repeats.

'In the centre of it all.'

'In the centre of it all,' he repeats in a whisper so quiet she doesn't hear him.

———

Coarse gritstone that knuckles its way out of the earth and sparkles in the sun soon becomes buff limestone. The sun paints patterns upon the rock from a different palette.

Where the land falls away they see great plunging slabs of pale stone the colour of a few drops of blood in a small bowl of water. Like the open wounds of the earth exposed.

The scars of the gods.

———

Later, crouched low in a copse that is a green fortress on the yellowing thirsty plains, the night is disturbed by sounds that scare them. Howls and screams, and once a low grunting of something close by, urgent and ravenous. The dogs and the swine are restless too so the man sits up to keep watch. He has his spear and he has his slingshot but neither are any use against the flies that flit around his head. He swats them away but each time many more return. He watches the woman, who is sleeping now on the dried beast's hide, curled on one side, and he feels something strong inside him, a feeling that keeps him warm through the cooling moments of night, a feeling of a need to protect but also a reliance upon her too, and he wonders if this will be the time, whether this trip will give them what they want, what they crave and desperately desire, whether adhering to the rituals and appeasing the gods in the centre of it all will bear bounty, and then he thinks about what he would do without her, and how without her he would be here all alone, just him and the beasts, and he is very scared and very awake.

───────

They first feel its pull.

They have felt it from down a dale, through a river and across several hills. They are aware of its proximity and then they finally come upon it, rising before them.

Perhaps they have been pulled towards it from the moment they left their home many mornings ago, for they know that such things are not built by chance.

Strategically placed at the peak of the land, there it is. A sacred circle of stones.

An avenue of rocks to guide them to it.

They see the smouldering remains of last night's fires first, the damp blue plumes of morning neglect.

They see the huts dotted around the place.

They see and hear and smell the animals that are corralled or tethered to posts – swine and oxen and cows and sheep and unfamiliar creatures that look like sheep but aren't sheep and in fact have blank eyes and faces that make them look more like people.

They see bowls, and tools for tilling and sowing, and bags of grain.

They see men and women. Many men and women, unfolding themselves towards the sun's embrace.

And they see the circle of stones in the centre of it all.

The stones stand straight and true like young trees. They grow from the soil, twelve of them arranged in as perfect a circle as a man could measure.

The woman notices they have been shaped and sculpted, these stones, and that they bear the scars and scuff marks of hammer and chisel. They are as similar and as different as people are to one another, twelve individuals belonging to a greater community; they have a commonality, a sense of belonging. There is a continuity in the way the circle goes on forever.

The man notices that beyond the circle's perimeter a trench has been dug, its contents used to create surrounding earthworks that act as protector to the monuments without obscuring them from view.

It all stands here for a reason too big to understand, yet they both know that they believe in the reason.

Each stone, thinks the woman, has a character, and none is to be feared. In fact, she wants nothing more than to touch them, and to walk to their centre, and to sit there, and feel the sky overhead, and the sun on her cheek, and then lie back and sleep deeply.

But there are other people here. Some look on, and one or two begin to wander over, and the dogs whine and gurgle, but the man tells them to be quiet, and still the woman does not feel fear.

She feels happiness, or something stronger, stranger.

A feeling beyond words.

———

A woman approaches them. She is tall and dark and is followed closely by another woman, who is even darker and more beautiful. They squint into the sunlight and then shade their eyes.

'We welcome you,' says the first. 'Do you farm?'

The man nods. 'We farm. Yes.'

'What do you bring to trade?'

'Swine, tools and skills. Seeds. And goodwill.'

The tall dark woman nods. She smiles.

'Do you stay here always?' asks the man.

'No one stays here always. But there is a place for you to rest.'

She points towards the huts that are scattered around the field beyond the stone circle. They look like large bowls woven from branches, upended and big enough to sleep two.

'There is a place for everyone,' adds the beautiful woman, but when she speaks they see that she has no teeth at all, and her voice is a soft rasp formed by the softness of her troubled mouth. 'If you have an offering.'

'We do,' says the woman. She points to one of the swine. 'We lost one on the way.'

'Or it was stolen,' adds the man.

'There is no stealing here,' says the tall woman.

'Good.'

'There is no killing here,' says the woman without teeth.

'We only want to appease the gods and receive our reward.'

'This is the place for that. This is the time for that.'

'That is what we heard,' says the woman. 'That is what we hoped.'

There is a moment's silence, and then the tall dark woman speaks.

'The swine must have a thirst.'

The man nods.

'And the dogs,' she says. 'You should rest before night.'

'Before night?' says the woman.

'Everything happens upside down here,' says the beautiful woman with no teeth. 'Upside down and inside out. Light is dark and dark is light. No days and no nights. Wrongways and gods-wise, all happens at sunrise.'

'There is water over there,' says the tall dark woman, pointing to a ditch.

The two women turn and walk away.

———

They sleep until just before sundown and awake to activity.

There is a crowd now, of people like them, men and women together, without children, farmers mainly, drawn from afar. They are gathering in clusters on the earthworks, by the ditch and in the stone circle, and already many processes of bartering and negotiation are underway. Transactions are taking place.

There is much to trade, laid out right there on the arid patch or, in the case of the animals, tethered close by. There are farmers offering seeds, bulbs and cuttings. Others have pigs, cows, sheep. Murderous hunting dogs and tiny puppies too. There are bitches in season, bitches for breeding. Stacks of baskets, sacks, purses and pouches to be swapped. Flint heads, spears, slingshots, cudgels. Swaddling clothes and bowls. Cured hides. Leather balls and spools of twine.

There are cheeses and balls of butter. Sides of pork and ham.

Nuts and dried fruit. Beans and lentils and flax.

Honey, oil, wax.

Not everything serves a practical purpose. Some offer small items to be enjoyed as luxuries, such as colourful stones and necklaces made from shells or animal skulls tinted purple with dyes made from berries. There are ornamental carvings from horn and bone. Woven head-bands. One woman is offering intricate hair plaits.

And in amongst the traders are several solitary men. They walk alone between and around the stones, and now and again they stop and pick up an object. They slap the haunch of a swine or check the teeth of a sheep.

They look at those who are trading and they exchange a word or two, sometimes more. Some just walk on by, saying nothing.

The man and the woman hastily wash the dust from the swine and let the curious dogs lead them to the marketplace.

They all draw interest – man, woman and animals alike.

They are viewed with similar wandering glances from the other trading farmers, but especially from several of the solitary men. One in particular watches from afar, half obscured by one of the large standing stones. The woman is distracted with the dogs but the man sees him and offers the smallest nod of the head. The man behind the stone just stares back.

———

Darkness is falling, though it is not true darkness, but instead the thin, charged light of the longest, brightest day, when the air appears to be stretched so tightly that it hums, and the grass rustles with life, and night never really presents itself, and is merely the day resting for a while.

The man who was lurking behind the stone slowly walks over and stands before them. They see that though he is short and his shoulders broad he has one arm that is small and withered. It has the dimensions of that of a small child. His chest and arms are thick with curled hairs that have turned a honey colour in the sun.

'What do you offer?' he asks.

When he speaks it is to both of them, though his eyes are trained on the woman.

The man gestures to the tethered swine.

'As many of those as you have fingers, less one to give to the gods.'

The hairy man looks at the animals. He crouches down and studies them closely.

'They could be fatter,' he says.

'They're the finest swine you'll ever taste,' says the woman, trying not to look at his arm. 'Feed a family for so many sunrises. See you right through the snow time. They're breeders too.'

The hairy man looks at her again. He looks her up and down in a way that makes her feel naked. Stares.

'What about those dogs?'

'What about them?' says the man.

'I'll need one to drive them.'

'Don't you have your own?'

He shakes his head.

'I come in what I wear. I carry all I need inside me.'

The man and the woman look at each other. The light is fading rapidly now. Without saying a word they know they are in silent agreement. This is what they have walked across the plains for. They have little choice.

'If you take the swine you can have one of the dogs.'

The hairy man considers the offer. Even though he knows he is going to accept it he prolongs his response.

He looks at the woman again and she feels her stomach turn sour.

'The swine and one dog is a fair exchange for what I have.'

'How are we to believe you?'

'Believe me?'

'How are we to believe it works?' says the woman.

'Have you appeased the gods fully?' says the hairy man with the small arm.

'Yes. Daily.'

'Then the gods know.'

'But how are we to know?'

He shrugs. 'Because today is the day when the sun shines brightest and longest, and at sunrise the world is born anew. Because I drink a bowl of pig's blood every day and I have done this many times before. Ask others.'

'Ask who?'

The hairy man looks around. He points to two men and a women. One of the men is bent over and packing away a stack of willow-branch baskets.

'We accept,' says the woman.

The hairy man nods to the centre of the stone circle.

'Then we pray to the gods and we wait,' says the hairy man. 'We wait until just before daylight.'

He looks at the man for a moment.

'Not you, though. Just me and her.'

Crouched once again in a copse, he watches as the first fingers of light curl around the edge of the night. Backlit, the clouds become illuminated.

He hears the tentative call of the first waking bird, a budding song still in search of a melody.

The tall dark woman and the beautiful woman with no teeth told him he had to leave and not return until the day was fully light and the dew had dried on the grass. They pointed to the trees and told him he could sleep there, and that he must not enter the stone circle. To do that would be to go against the gods. To go against the gods would spoil the ritual for everyone. And the ritual happens but twice a year; on the longest, brightest day of sun and the shortest, darkest day of ice.

They could not guarantee his safety if he disturbed the ritual.

He is hungry but he cannot eat. He is thirsty but he dare not lift a cup to wet his lips. Instead he is crouched like a banished creature in a dark corner of the copse, unmoving.

And now he sees the first shaft of light pierce a cloud like a bone needle through cowhide. It shines straight between two of the standing stones and directly into the centre of the stone circle. The light and the stones are perfectly aligned.

Even from this distance he see shapes; the shapes of bodies twisting and writhing.

Many of them tangled in union.

As the sun strengthens, the beam stays trained on the circle, and its warming rays widen to bathe it entirely in glorious life-giving light.

She is somewhere in there.

The hairy man is upon her and he is holding her. His shrunken arm is surprisingly strong as he adeptly turns her over and arranges her. She is only half aware of the movements from the others within the circle but the sounds are difficult to ignore. The moaning, the sobbing. The grunting. Her knees are sore on the hard dry ground, and he has his hands in her hair and his breath in her ear. She can smell him. As she feels the rising sun warm her back she gives herself to him, to the ritual. To the gods. She closes her eyes and drifts somewhere else, and for a while time slips away and then it feels as if many hands are on her, as if many fingers are running through her hair, grabbing at it and knotting it around a hand or many hands. There are mouths on her. All over, hot, wet mouths. It is as if she is being touched, inside and out, and the moaning and the sobbing and the grunting is loud now, and it is all around, and she is surprised to hear that she is moaning and sobbing and grunting too, and the sun is rising and burning and moiling. Light spreads across the circle and the stones cast long shadows like contorted creatures and colours swirl behind her eyes, but she refuses to open them. She is being pushed and pulled, and there are hands and mouths upon her, and her back is burning and the colours are swirling, and there is laughter and screams and howls and whimpers and the sound of bellowing, and the shadows bend and stretch as the sun encircles them, and they are all at its centre as seeds take root in the soil of longing. And the gods grant them their wishes.

———

There is still a frost on the ground, and the first shoots of spring have not yet pushed through the frozen carpet that covers the soil, as she lies in agony in the shadowed shell of the cave.

He is by her side, with a stick for her to bite down on, and water, and the fire is blazing. He has enough wood stacked so that it could burn for days. There is food too. He has made the correct preparations.

The woman's legs are wide apart and she faints from the pain but when she comes around the head is there, poking out, a small dark wet dome of thick hair, and then two eyes are peeking out at the world, seeking a light for guidance.

She screams and the baby slithers out on to the bed of moss.

The dog pads over and tries to lick the child free of the slick film that covers it but the man slaps it away. The baby is silent but breathing.

He wipes its face and crouches down to bite the cord. And that is when he sees it in the half-light made by the flicker of flames: one arm so small it is almost unreal.

The child gurgles and opens its eyes. It reaches out for him.

He extends a finger and the child's tiny digits curl around it.

They grip.

Suburban Animals

Before everything.

Before anxiety stalked the fallow meadows of our adult minds, there was adolescence: that time trap between bodies old and new, when innocence was a commodity, a virtue.

We lived in the suburbs and the suburbs seemed to go on forever. Nothing but mile after mile of tarmac and culs-de-sac curving around dead-end corners. Low houses with double-glazed windows that reflected vapour trails as they cross-hatched the young summer sky marked the limit of our world, the only one we knew. We occupied these spaces entirely.

Suburbia: a combination of the words *suburb* and *utopia*; each iteration different, yet somehow the same. Ours was a microcosm of houses built from the same blueprint, outside of which waxed cars sat gleaming on new driveways laid by a team of travellers who had come from a campsite up near Consett to resurface half the estate several seasons earlier. Hundreds of houses sported the same sets of vertical blinds in their living room windows too, sold to the owners by a single salesman on a winning streak.

Here we roamed a labyrinth of post-war new-builds constructed for an emerging lower middle class, a place promising minimal crime, green spaces and easy access to motorways taking you to Edinburgh or London, Sunderland or St-Tropez.

There was a shopping precinct, playing fields and endless alleyways hosting outdated graffiti slowly fading from view like a pavement artist's chalk masterpiece in the rain. There was a church for believers, a rest home for the elderly and a graveyard waiting to be filled.

Beyond the houses, where creosote-stained fences demarcated the struggle between new suburban and old rural, lay wheat fields, and beyond the wheat fields were more estates where once there had been old parish villages devoted to the mining of coal. These further-flung conurbations mirrored our lives from across the scrublands. And stalking the perimeter of the estate, leafy lanes provided deep cover for day-long games and the covert depositing of secret stashes of pornography.

We had gardens, we had trees, we had freedom.

There was little wildlife in the suburbs, though. No foxes or squirrels or badgers or deer, just soft cats and overfed dogs.

And people.
Suburban animals.

———————

We were playing cricket on the school fields during the holidays when Duncan was bowled out by his brother Luke.

Duncan was two years older than the rest of us, and had been born with Down's syndrome. He liked to ride his bike to my house without using the pedals, preferring to power along with his feet in great loping strides.

The brothers came from a loving family. Their parents were older than the rest of ours, and Christians, but they didn't press the point. And Duncan was not *special* or *tapped*. He was simply one of us.

But he had his rituals, and one of his favourites was that every time he was bowled out in a game of cricket he would snatch the stumps from the soil and hurl them at anyone within reach. What began once in a fit of genuine anger had now turned into a game in which we all had to yell 'Duncan – *no!*' as three sharpened stumps came flying towards our heads, and Duncan guffawed with delight.

Sometimes he liked to drop his trousers and wave his oversized cock about. Duncan had hit puberty before the rest of us, and was covered in hair down there. Thick, dark tangles of it. A mass of tiny wires. It was hard not to look, if only to see what lay ahead for us; he might have had to go to a different school, and would live a shorter life, but Duncan had a larger, hairier appendage and was playing his young adulthood to his advantage.

———————

After a morning on the open fields we'd moved over to the all-weather football pitch, whose AstroTurf could take the skin clean off a knee and leave a red-raw medallion shape beneath your stonewashed jeans if you mistimed a sliding tackle.

The ball was being lazily hoofed about when the boys appeared. There were three of them, the same age as Duncan. They came on to the pitch and sauntered over, snatching the ball from mid-air. Duncan tried to grab it back but they passed it to one another in a way designed to make him look foolish, and suddenly the summer's day had cracks in its blue-glazed veneer. In that moment I wished that we had the cricket stumps to hand, so that Duncan's inhibitions might prompt him to skewer one of their skulls.

Any young boy knows that such cliques rely on power, and the power in this group lay in Kyle Todd, an indulged boy with hair so blonde he could almost pass for an albino. He often rode new BMX bikes, each latest model replacing the last, sported expensive trainers and carried himself with the confidence of someone who, superficially at least, was treated as royalty at home, but who was now taking those parental shortcomings out on anyone who was smaller, younger or happier than him.

Duncan's anger was rising, and when that happened he wore it on the soft round features of his face, his hands slowly curling into fists and his cheeks flushing plum. Luke and I advanced to try and get the ball back, but before we reached them Toddsy bounced it off Duncan's head and the three of them roared with laughter. We heard the noise the ball made and then Duncan wail out of frustration rather than pain. Even at twelve, the rest of us could see that this was a predictable scene from a high school morality film, but we also knew we had to see it through to the inevitable conclusion. That fact was inescapable.

The ball rolled away and I bent to retrieve it, but one of the other boys punted it way down to the other end of the pitch.

Somewhere far away a car alarm was going off, insistent but ignored and therefore entirely ineffective. I also heard a bird, a seagull, though we were miles from the sea.

The boys started taunting Duncan with words you know but don't need to see written down; words that split the sanctity of the suburbs. They made mocking gestures that years later an American presidential candidate would make on live television and still be voted in by the electorate. Gestures that further cracked the carapace of our childhoods. Toddsy swigged from a can of Coke, and spat some of it in our direction. It dribbled down his stupid chin.

We asked them to stop, pulled Duncan back. We led him away, back to our ball, to our game, to our summer.

Smirking and drooling, Toddsy turned and left, his honking lickspittle lackeys following in swaggering pursuit.

———

We calmed Duncan down, threw our damp T-shirts to the ground and got a kick-about going, but the boys were still there, lurking in the dark corner of the pitch in a tight huddle of sharp laughter and raging hormones. The chain-link fence that surrounded the pitch as if it were a prison yard cast a curious shadow on the fake green turf, and I could see what they were doing back there: Toddsy was urinating into the Coke can. They all were, one after the other.

I whistled to Luke and nodded in their direction. Noted the development.

We carried on with our game, and the heat prickled on unblemished skin turning pink in the first flush of holiday time. Duncan scored a belter in the imaginary top corner and did his customary celebration of a long lap of honour, with one arm outstretched and a finger pointing to the sky. His smile was as bright as the sun, life-giving. We laughed along with him.

Then the boys returned. Toddsy returned.

Now his arm was extended.

'Duncan,' he said, 'we brought a drink for you.'

He was offering the can to him.

'Don't take it, Duncan,' said Luke.

'He's pissed in it,' I said.

And the thing with Duncan was, if you said not to do something, he did it. That's just the way it was. Same with the cricket stumps. Same with jumping off the shed roof. Same with dropping an empty glass bottle on to the cracked stone flags of the shopping precinct. With Duncan, *don't* meant *do*. It wasn't a problem; it just meant a little explaining or cleaning up for Luke afterwards. It was Duncan's way and he was one of us.

I could see where some of the warm piss had missed the hole in the top of the can and pooled in the little declivity around the rim. It was quite dark in colour; the tone of a hot day. It wasn't cola. It definitely wasn't that.

The three lads were leering, and Duncan was grinning. He wanted their gift. He knew he couldn't have it, and he wanted it more than anything.

'Don't, Duncan.'

Don't meant *do*.

Toddsy continued to hold the can out. An offering. The gap between him and Duncan – between Duncan and the can – narrowed and there were no gulls or planes in the sky now. There was not even a solitary cloud, just a deep-blue bank of endless summer, as if the universe beyond it were entirely empty, and someone somewhere on the estate was mowing a lawn to keen precision.

Time slowed, spooled away towards mythology. There was Toddsy and there was Duncan and there was the warm can of urine. Duncan laughed. He chuckled.

'Here you go, have a drink on us,' said Toddsy.

Duncan advanced. Flanked by his friends, Toddsy gestured with the can. Invited him. Urged him.

'Go on.'

Now we were all shouting: 'Duncan, don't.'

Don't meant *do*.

Duncan reached out for the can and he took it.

He took the can of piss and he smiled as he raised it to his lips and had a sip, a gulp, and as he did Luke leaped forward and yelled out – 'Duncan – *no!*' – and he slapped it from his big brother's hand. It landed on the ground between Duncan and Toddsy, and its contents glugged on to the coarse green plastic of the fake football pitch.

The sun beat down and no one said anything. Instead 'Duncan – *no!*' hung there, filling the silence between us. Those two words were weighted with feeling; weighted with anger and brotherly love and horror and cruelty. They were a single sound rising from deep within, the sound of the thin shell of innocence shattering forever.

———

After everything.

After we grew into men and went out into the world, to jobs and wives and children, I looked up Toddsy on

Facebook. After more than thirty years it took less than five seconds to locate him.

He runs a business laying patios in Sunderland. He has kids. I found his address online and I visited his house on Google Maps. It is a red-brick new-build in the style of a faux-townhouse. I have dragged and dropped the yellow icon on Street View and I've stood outside it. I've positioned myself at the bottom of his driveway. I've zoomed in on the windows. I've found the room in which he sleeps.

On my computer screen the sun is shining and the day is bright, just like it was all those years ago. The street sits beneath another rare clear blue sky, once again so devoid of cloud as to be almost unreal.

The house is not far from the sea.

I think I hear seagulls.

The Whip Hand

The waltzer ground to a premature halt for the first time that summer.

The ride screeched, juddered angrily and finally sighed. The spinning cars slowly came to a standstill on their tilted axes and the screams of the riders faded away in their tight young throats. Without the accelerated action of movement to accompany it, the pulsing electro music that pumped out of the speakers and echoed across the half-empty showground alongside the operator's stock set of phrases – *Hold tight, here we go!* – suddenly seemed hollow and banal.

Beneath the running boards, on a shaded patch of sun-starved grass that had turned an acidic yellow, Walt Moody lay half pulled into the cogs and axels of the machinery, dragged there like a helpless rag doll. One entire hand, wrist and arm were gone. Processed into a paste. His shoulder had been sucked in too but it was the big bone joint that connected his limb to his torso that had caused the greasy cogs to jam and the power switch to trip.

He had died in silence, a grease gun in his remaining hand and torn strips of oily rags hanging from his belt loops. A tailor-made cigarette hung suspended from his lower lip for a moment, still smoking, then fell to the parched turf. Here Walt Moody lay in the receding days of a long arid summer, pulped and pooling on dry soil split from a prolonged drought.

The ride that had brought him a small fortune, and helped make the Moodys one of the most famous showground families in England, had consumed him.

———

The funeral drew close to two thousand mourners.

Walt's eldest son and heir to the family's fairground empire, the notorious Whitey Moody, delayed the big day until season's end so that show folk could journey great distances to pay their respects to one of the old-timers. Representatives from all the oldest show folk families were in attendance. From Kent and Cambridgeshire they came. From Derbyshire and Gloucestershire. Some travellers even came over from Ireland.

It was a two-day send-off held right there on the showground, with flowers and foaming kegs of beer, eulogies and shared memories, fist fights and sing-songs, and a roaring bonfire whose smoke dried the damp eyes of many the entire weekend long.

On the night of the second day, deep in the ale and cider, Whitey Moody stood and made a heartfelt declaration to anyone who would listen.

'I will honour this man,' he said, pointing to a framed photograph of his father that he held aloft, 'he that built an empire from nothing; a man who has entertained generations, given pleasure to millions.'

The mourners and drinkers who surrounded the fire quietened down and listened, for when Whitey Moody spoke it was always with a flourish and a flair for drama. His oratory skills were renowned and few ever dared to talk over him.

'A humble fellow, my father. A small man with a big heart – and a great vision. So I will honour him with something great too. Hear this now: to Walter Moody I will erect a monument.'

His accent was geographically unidentifiable and linguistically nebulous, a hybrid of traveller cant and colloquial argot; that of a man perpetually on the move.

'I will climb the biggest hill and I will build it with my own hands,' he said. 'A stone sculpture to stand for centuries. Yes. A reminder of who this man was and what he represented. And for those of you who don't know, that was hard work, charity, generosity – and family. Especially family. Walter Moody was a god among men, and like a true god he will be honoured.'

As he talked, the glow from the hissing fire lit Whitey Moody's features from below. It accentuated the triangular shapes of his cheekbones and pronounced a mouth that appeared overcrowded by his strong equine teeth. It drew shadows down amongst his weathered creases and around the sunken pits of his wide eyes. Eyes that could reduce a man.

Most of all, the flickering orange light turned the brilliant blonde strands of his hair, now pulled back and thinning across his pate into a trademark ponytail – and for which he had earned a nickname so longstanding that few knew his birth name – magnesium in colour.

In the fire's glare every muscle of his short, taut body, every cord, seemed coiled in readiness for the task ahead.

'Now,' he said, 'who's with me?'

———

The wooded slopes stretched the length of the remote valley, up to a crest where the jagged treeline scratched at the turbid sky.

A motorcade of vehicles moved along the rutted track in a slow procession, tilting through potholes and edging over discarded, rotting lumber or tangled sprigs of fallen branches.

Leading from the front in a flatbed truck loaded with tools, tents and provisions was Whitey Moody. Behind him followed his younger brother, Joss Moody, who steered a battered old Land Rover with a large horse-box in tow. At the rear of the procession was a Transit driven by a showground hand known only as The Pole, an Eastern European war veteran hired three summers earlier and kept on by the Moodys for his strength, loyalty and mute menace. His cargo was human: a motley menagerie of men in various states of drunkenness and disrepair, collectively press-ganged, coerced, intimidated or snatched from smoky back rooms, parole-board halfway houses, gambling dens and the comfort of their beds across the north of England in the dead of night.

There were ten in all, and each indebted to the Moody family one way or another, for their business enterprises stretched beyond fairgrounds and into arcades, cafes, seaside promenade palm-reading booths, betting shops, card games, cattle trading, terrier breeding, dog tracks and an under-the-radar loan business. Those who had failed to repay their longstanding debts or had inadvertently crossed the Moodys – smashing a fruit machine in a fit of anger, perhaps, or attempting to rig a poker game – now found themselves having to compensate in a most unexpected way.

The track petered out into a clearing where the remnants of a logging operation were still visible: ragged stumps, a blackened fire circle, crushed beer cans.

The dense woodlands spread in all directions, the timber trunks and latticework of bare branches cutting light to a minimum.

Whitey Moody climbed down from his truck and stared deep into the trees, and for a moment the wood was as still and hallowed a space as a church. A rug of needles lay underfoot, their tips the colour of rust.

Somewhere in the distance a well-fed pheasant clumsily took flight from the undergrowth, clattering through the corridor of spindly columns and rising up into the air with neither style nor grace.

He turned back to the men as they unfolded themselves from the vehicles, and spoke.

'You might as well get yourselves comfortable, lads. No one leaves until the job gets done.'

'What job?' said one of the men.

Whitey Moody turned back to the trees again, squinting up the steep slopes to the crest of the vale. Here he saw landslides of shale and stone. He saw undulations and craggy protrusions; knuckles of rock the size of small buildings.

He said nothing.

———

The horsebox had been fitted with bunks to sleep on, and two large circular canvas military tents were erected either side of it. A bleating lamb was tethered to the tow bar of the flatbed truck, on which there was also a cage of chickens. A large bonfire was built and lit.

The men stood around it, absorbing the heat, sullen and uncertain. Fearful. The soft wet loam beneath their feet felt unusual and the strange full-throated croak of a pair of nesting ravens nearby was like no sound they had heard before.

Joss Moody circled the fire and handed each man a boiler suit and a woollen hat. The Pole followed, passing each man two raw sausages, a bread roll and a can of beer. Some of them tentatively scouted for sticks on which to roast their dinner. Unsure, others loitered. One or two of the more hardened drinkers swapped their sausages for an extra can.

Soon there was the sound of pork fat hissing on glowing coals and the murmurs of men crouched low on their haunches as the sun began to sink below the treeline.

Wearing only a vest, Whitey Moody emerged from the horsebox. He held a number of pairs of handcuffs and folded over one arm was a length of chain.

'See these?' he said, rattling the cuffs. 'These are for those that reckon on leaving. So pipe up now if you're planning on that.'

No man spoke.

'And don't be thinking of taking off in the night either,' he added. 'It's a good ten-mile clip to the nearest town. Thirty to the nearest train station. We'll be after you with dogs before you've cleared a woodland mile.'

He let the threat settle.

'Good, then,' he said. 'Follow me.'

He took an overgrown trail thick with brambles where the only footprints were the two-toed markings of deer hooves. They arrived at a smaller clearing. In the centre were three large blocks of rough-cut granite, each about a metre across.

'Right,' said Whitey Moody. 'This is what's happening. You lot are going to take these and shift them up there.'

Here he pointed up through the woods to the top of the hill, a hundred metres or more away.

'You'll stack them and when that's done I'll get the whole lot engraved in remembrance of my father, Walter Moody. Until that time, you're mine.'

'Those blocks must weigh a tonne,' said one of the men.

'Nearly three, as it happens,' said Joss Moody. '*Each*.'

'We'll never be able to move them.'

Whitey strode over to the man who had spoken, a young sneak thief from Glasgow, and grabbed him by the front of his boiler suit. He slapped him once, hard. The sound of open palm on the young man's cheek echoed through the still wood.

'You can and you will,' he said. 'If the Egyptians could build the pyramids, Whitey Moody can get three bloody blocks up a hill in England.'

One of the other men cleared his throat and then tentatively spoke.

'Mr Moody, sir.'

Whitey turned to him. 'What?'

'I just wondered, how do you propose we do it?'

'With muscle and might,' he said. 'With brains and brawn, lad. With ropes and pulleys and rollers. With generators and chains. With whatever it takes to get the job done. There's food and shelter and more ale than any of you could hope to ever drink for those that prove themselves. Our Joss has done a fresh batch. Isn't that right, brother?'

Beside him Joss nodded.

'A right good sup,' he said. 'It'll make you see God and want to kiss his feet. It'll blow your head-handles clean off.'

'And what about those that don't want to work?' said the young Glaswegian, a man barely out of his teens.

Whitey turned to him again.

'You're testing my patience, son.'

'And he's not a patient man,' said Joss.

'I just wondered, though,' said the Scotsman.

'It's simple,' said Whitey. 'There's a spade and plenty of soil for you to dig it with. You want to make sure the hole is deep, though, so the foxes don't get at you when The Pole here puts you under. They say it's worse than drowning, being buried alive. The dirt gets everywhere. Fills every hole. The worms and insects too. Oh, and the maggots. They get in there and start eating at you from the inside.'

Whitey Moody looked at the rest of the men. He saw the fear on their faces and he was pleased. Fear was what would fuel them onwards.

He sniffed.

'You best get started, then.'

The next day was spent hefting granite and slipping in unforgiving sod.

Hands became first blistered and then callused. The men argued amongst themselves and nearly came to blows several times, only to be separated by The Pole, who did not utter a single word.

As they worked, Whitey went off to check the snares he had set the night before. He returned an hour later with a half-dozen rabbits, strung through the heel on a line, and already becoming stiff with rigor mortis.

He sat on an alder stump and set about gutting the animals, their entrails thrown sizzling on to the fire. With a series of incisions and two large jerks he turned each of their pelts inside out and then hung them from branches. On a block of wood he butchered the rabbits and then dropped their parts into a large stew pot. Thigh, leg, torso. Haunch. He added potatoes, carrots, cabbage. Salt.

By the sun's setting the men had moved one block of granite twenty feet across the soil under the watchful eye of Joss Moody.

They ate well that night, then retired to their tents and horsebox. In the darkness they whispered about the possibility of escaping to their wives and girlfriends and children. They talked about overpowering their captors and taking flight, and letting the moonlight guide the way.

In the morning a skein of frost had tightened across the soft soil and made furrows of their footprints and the track marks left by the dragged block. They were awoken early, given tea and a tin of fruit each, and then sent to work on the slopes all day. Lunch was leftover rabbit stew. Tea was boiled eggs, bread and beer.

The granite block was dragged up the slopes first with ropes and felled trunks acting as rollers, and then, where the slope steepened up towards a sky that was now streaked with the first incoming frosted fingers of winter, via a series of steps dug into the earth.

The men worked this way for two weeks. They slept and ate. They defecated into a pit and they washed themselves in a flooded ditch deep with copper-coloured bog water. They still talked about escaping back to their homes and hovels but it had become an abstract idea, as they now believed Whitey Moody to be a man of his word. They understood that Whitey Moody had the whip hand.

———

Snow fell on the day that they heaved the first block of granite up to the lip of the valley and out on to the peak of the hill. Here the men slumped to the ground, their muscles aching in sweat-soaked boiler suits now stale and pungent.

The peak was a small area of scrub thick with brambles, through which a small patch had been cleared to make way for the monument.

Only when they stood and stretched did the men see the view.

The countryside ran in all directions, a series of layers and levels, the land a laminated space of dales and delphs, vales and valleys, their uppermost edges dusted in the first tentative snowfall. It was like a dream. They became silent, their chests rising and falling as they gulped in the cold metallic air of an English winter.

'Not there,' said Whitey. He pointed to a patch six feet further along. '*There*.'

The men groaned.

'Can't we take a minute for a gasper, Mr Moody?'

This was said by a stout ex-boxer from Norfolk who now made a living taking on all-comers in a tent on the Moody funfair. His crime had been to fight in a showcase bout at McGintey's Pleasure Palace in Blackpool during the off-season. His work for a rival family had cost him several weeks of his life – and two crushed fingers.

'Aye, I expect you can,' said Whitey Moody. He reached into his pocket and pulled out a pack of cigarettes. 'Pass them round,' he said. 'Go on: smoke yourselves silly.'

The men lit up and stood inhaling and exhaling in silence, the canopy of trees below them dotted with the bladed crowns of crow's nests swaying in the scaffold of the thinnest branches and the slopes rolling downwards to where a twist of grey smoke spiralled upwards from their camp.

'It's beautiful,' said a voice. It could have been any one of the men speaking, for they were all sharing this same thought. 'Bloody beautiful.'

The second stone took ten days to heave up the hill.

Across the woods the snow lay thick on the ground now. It changed the shape of the landscape. Levelled it in places. It shortened contours and erased hollows. Muted the woodland noises.

The dirty circle of the camp was still visible from up on the crest of the valley, a trampled target of tiny footprints with the firepit its bullseye. Then, leading from it, a narrow dark streak of mud running up the hill like a road to the sky.

Whitey joined the men putting his shoulder to the stone. Joss too.

They were all gaining strength now. The men's bodies were changing. Tightening. The clean air, exercise and fresh meat and vegetables that Whitey brought them meant many were experiencing the first balanced diets of their lives. Save for beer and cigarettes, their other vices had been forcefully curtailed.

Naturally there were arguments and several fist fights, one of them organised as evening entertainment for which the contenders received a cash payment from Whitey, and during which a nose was broken and several knuckles left crooked, but the combatants shook hands at the end.

One evening, after the stone had been dug into the earth and held fast with driven stakes and chains lagged to nearby trees, Whitey Moody left the camp with a pair of bolt cutters. He was gone all night and returned at first light with a gash on his forehead, a generator, two drums of diesel and his young nephew, Frankie Moody.

The firstborn of Whitey's second sister, Francine, Frankie Moody had the same blonde hair as his uncle, near-albino in colour, and he too worked the fairgrounds as a humper and handyman. At sixteen he already had the physique of an older man, and a scowl that suggested he feared no one, not least a rag-tag press gang of men.

Frankie took to tinkering with the generator. On the second day he stepped back, put his toolbox to one side and started it up. It coughed three times like an emphysemic old man lighting up his first phlegm-cutter of the day and then sputtered into action, the mechanical *put-put* sound of it echoing up through the woods. There was a small cheer from those watching men who knew that their workload was now halved.

The generator was soon set up to turn a cable wheel to hoist the stone up the final few metres of the bank.

———

That night Whitey let the men finish early.

'Get yourself scrubbed up,' he said. 'We're going out.'

The men looked at each other.

'But we *are* out?' said one.

'We're going *out* out,' he replied. 'Out of these bloody woods.'

'You mean we're going home?'

'I already told you: you go home when the job gets done. I'm taking you out on the town.'

At this, the men were unsure how to react.

'You're allowed to crack a bloody smile, you know,' said Whitey. 'Me, I'm off for a feed and a right big drink.'

'Really, Mr Moody?'

'Look lively. We leave in ten minutes.'

The men climbed into the Transit and on to the back of the flatbed and left. Only The Pole stayed behind to watch over the camp.

They ploughed through the woods as the trees on either side hung heavy with thick pillows of snow. The night was still and clear as their vehicles rolled and stalled and the men shivered.

After a time they turned into an old cart track and then that widened into a logging road and then soon the logging road plunged them towards civilisation. They drove on, passing farmsteads, hamlets and villages, and then they were at the edge of a town.

The men marvelled at the neon lights, the traf-fic and the sharp angles of the buildings that grew tall around them. They saw lamp posts and over-lit offices. Garage forecourts and flyovers. Multi-storey car parks and dark underpasses. It all seemed such a contrast to the trees and mud and snow of the past few weeks.

They parked at a fast food restaurant. They ordered burgers and fries, Cokes and milkshakes. Whitey paid. When they had eaten they ordered more burgers and more fries. More drinks. When they finished those they ordered the same again. Apple pies and doughnuts too. Ice cream. Teas and coffees. Then they sat back and yawned and belched and lit cigarettes and sat smoking until the night manager nervously asked the men to leave. Whitey Moody pushed a ten-pound note into the manager's breast pocket and gently slapped his face. The men roared with laughter at this, and spilled out into the night in their own time, a million stars above them, their bellies full to swelling, and their heads reeling with possibility.

This strange alliance walked to the nearest pub, where they drank beer and whiskey. They played pool and commandeered the jukebox. They smoked cigarettes, and cigars too, and Whitey and Joss Moody joined in with the jokes and singing. Then they moved to another pub, and then another.

They found themselves in a nightclub. Here they got each other in friendly headlocks and they tried to talk to women, and they staggered around a dance floor beneath a flickering strobe light. They spilled drinks and then when the house lights came up one or two of the younger men had passed out on tables, and the others lifted them up and carried them out, singing and laughing into the sub-zero night.

Hungover but reinvigorated, the next morning the men gave a galvanised push on the third stone to be laid in testament to Walter Moody. They worked until lunchtime, Whitey barking orders and conducting the operation.

When they returned to camp, The Pole had slaughtered the lamb that had been fattening for weeks, and mounted it on a stick. It spat globs of fat on to the glowing ash below. They dined on great hunks of it then returned to the slopes.

It was dusk and the stone just fifteen feet from the top of the hill when the securing cable snapped and its tangle of moorings came whipping through the air like a lightning bolt of steel. The generator upended and there was an almighty rumble.

'*Run.*'

The men scattered as the piece of granite bore down on them, a growing blot against the fading sun.

Whitey slipped in the morass. He flailed, then fell.

The stone bounced once and then twice and then it rolled right over him. It crushed him in an instant, then carried on down the hill, where it butted up against a craggy outcrop with a loud crack that resonated across the valley.

Joss Moody scrambled through the snow and mud and stooped to where his brother lay prone, his body broken but the strong features of his face somehow untouched by the tumbling granite.

The men hurried to join him.

Joss hesitated, uncertain, his face wracked with grief and horror. His chest rising and falling.

Silence reigned.

Then Joss slowly straightened. He gathered his breath. Composed himself.

'Hear this now,' he said. 'A great man has passed today. My brother Whitey Moody is dead. And I will honour him.'

There was another long silence before a voice spoke.

'How, Joss?'

'I will erect a monument to him,' he replied. 'One to stand tall on the skyline here in these woods right next to that of his father, Walt Moody. And you will all help me.'

The Last Apple Picker

He first arrived at the orchard uninvited. Early September. Here in a field of cowslip he pitched his tent and helped with the apple picking.

The man said little, asked for nothing. He dined on bread and windfall, bathed in the top pond. Sometimes he tended to the trees too, cutting away the parasitic creepers that slowly strangled everything living.

Then, when the branches were stripped of their perennial bounty and the barrels brimming, and the wind blew in on a westerly, without a word he left, a yellowing patch of grass where once he slept.

The next year he returned, and kept returning, each time a little older, a little thinner, to slowly toss the ancient gleaming apples down to the soft carpet of the orchard and swat away wasps that feasted on those decaying fruit too sour to keep.

After a decade or so the farmer's wife offered him the barn and a bath, but he politely refused. He preferred the tent, the pond. The field of cowslip.

Another decade passed this way until one autumn he did not appear.

The harvest was particularly poor that year; the trees were covered in ivy and the crop infested with worms. It was as if the orchard were in mourning for its quiet custodian.

That winter three trees were felled in a storm and the farmer suffered first financial difficulty and then a tragedy too great to allow him to think about things as small as apples.

In time the orchard itself was gone.

But deep in the soil the seeds of fallen apples sat silently awaiting sunlight.

Saxophone Solos

The transition from reader-cum-fan to the world's leading authority on Bill Katz and organiser of an international academic symposium devoted to his eleven novels and three collections of essays and journalism, to then latterly becoming his lover, was as steady a trajectory as it was predictable, the type of narrative arc that Dr Elizabeth Brownlee herself would be the first to dismiss as the redundant remains of that precious strand of fiction that used to sell rather well up until ten or fifteen years ago.

If she had read it as an abstract for a conference or a submission to the literary anthology she co-edited, she would surely have rejected it without hesitation.

What had once been an illicit liaison that buckled under the pressure of its own inevitability had now hardened into a hollow relationship that echoed with the tinny callbacks of centuries of literary cliché, yet still she allowed herself to become the chief antagonist in the drama of this publicly recognisable writer's well-documented private life, the person some deemed responsible (though, of course, the responsibility was all his) for finally ending his marriage to the television producer and mother of his two children, Anne Allan.

The whole thing was sordid and embarrassing for all concerned, except, perhaps, for Katz himself. Led by his waning libido and pathetically grateful for the attention from a bright woman on the right side of not-too-young, he saw this development as the unexpected opening of the penultimate act of a career that had seen him slip from the eloquent bad boy of digestible liberal intellectualism in the 1990s to the midlist novelist of the late 2010s.

A thin layer of scandal in an era in which the old, deeply rooted totems of patriarchy were falling hard and fast around him was, he reasoned, a minor act of rebellion, perhaps his very last. It was one final stab at the type of mischief that kept him in the gossip columns even when his paperback sales were beginning to scrape mid-to-low four figures.

He had done little to hide the affair, from either his wife or the hacks and bloggers who still begrudgingly devoted an inch or two to a writer of satire who'd once boasted of having taken acid with the current home secretary while they were postgraduates. Katz clung to this reputation of self-elected bon viveur for the middle-brow masses, quite unaware that his readership had grown up and moved out of the city that he still eulogised, and now lived in tall houses in Hastings, Totnes or Hebden Bridge that were full of retro turntables, spiralisers and cynical children, while he festered in a damp house south of the river.

He still smoked cigarettes, even though no one old smoked cigarettes any more. Yet there he was at prize-giving ceremonies, book launches (his, mainly) or out on the lecture circuit, standing on town hall balconies or huddled on rainy campus forecourts, puffing away with the young vapers, sporting ash smudges on his lapels with a misdirected sense of pride, like badges of honour that said: *I've still got it.*

Anne had left him several times before. On the last occasion she had cited, only half-jokingly to anyone who asked, that it was his love of music featuring saxophone solos that had killed it for her. 'When a man is tired of sax solos, he is tired of life,' he took to saying far too frequently, often to the same few people.

She had never quite worked out whether this particular penchant for seventies yacht rock and mainstream eighties power ballads that was defined by the incessant wailing of this tragically phallic instrument was genuine, or instead a commitment to a wider plan to grind her down. Either way, in Bill Katz's hands and on his stereo, the saxophone had been weaponised and turned into a tool of torture deployed in a kind of aural long game to provoke first irritation, then resentment, before segueing nicely into a divorce that, all being well, wouldn't wipe him out entirely.

It had worked, and Anne despised him for it just enough for her husband to feel validated and vindicated in pursuing this relationship with Dr Elizabeth Brownlee, though of the myriad real reasons for his ill-behaviour towards his wife it was perhaps the simple prevailing fact that she had recently been enjoying a more financially and critically successful career in film production, while his own was clearly faltering.

His last work, a thin novella that ostensibly appeared to be about a man who falls out of a tree, had barely made an impact, despite his genius agent somehow leveraging a commendable advance. Even Katz himself knew that this was unsustainable, especially as the many film and TV options that had been bubbling away on the back burner for the past decade had all but run dry, and he was now facing a fate worse than death: a possible return to a type of journalism that he no longer recognised, that of listicles and clickbait opinion pieces.

He shuddered at the prospect of dogged 10p-per-word provocation, when once his colourful behaviour had been the very source of the manufactured outrage.

He exhaled smoke across the restaurant table into the face of Dr Elizabeth Brownlee, who, after writing a thesis and several papers on the man and his work, and having organised the aforementioned three-day symposium at which Katz had made a surprise and somewhat smug appearance that featured an entrance choreographed with all the pomp of Liberace rising from his glittery grave to play one more encore on the Strip, suddenly realised that she was already sick of him. This epiphany finally came eight or nine months after he'd first put his hand on the back of her neck and gently caressed her there with two fingers that she thought felt cold, clammy and intrusive, as 'Born to Run' played through the cheap laptop speakers that he had set up beside some tea-light candles in his Novotel room.

What good fortune, he thought, gazing at her.

What disappointment, she thought back.

Vienna (*The Hunters in the Snow*)

I feel a fire inside, warming. Warming and burning.

Burning and blazing.

It comes on soon after we unfold our stiff, sleeping bodies and set out into the frozen blackness. A hundred crunching steps or less and the flames are licking at our chests, our throats gasping from the challenge of the snow-covered inclines steepening towards a sullen half-moon, the smoke of us pluming from our slack wet mouths. The wind means no candle lamp can light the way.

We chase the day.

Pray for prey.

Perhaps our prayers will be answered as thin limbs of light start to streak the dark and we walk and walk, searching for signs, and in the soft wakening sun the ashen sky feels as heavy as a laden sow. A net of snow suspended. There is surely more of it to fall. Deeper, thicker.

We walk into it.

Our hotel room was illuminated by lights that dangled from the high ceiling and had black bowler hats for lampshades that made me think of Magritte.

Plastic candles dripping simulacrum wax lined the stairs that led to the hushed corridor when we arrived late, tired from the flight and still carrying the faint scent of airline meals and stale pressurised cabin air. Though the corner room overlooked a busy junction, the windows were so well insulated against the cold that the horns of the passing trams and general traffic of Vienna were kept silent beneath layers of glass and a beautiful old set of heavy wooden shutters.

The hotel occupied one floor of a townhouse, and was discreetly run so as to give a homely feel to its visitors that my wife and I welcomed; there were no corporate-chain intrusions here, no unwanted muzak or unexpected add-ons to bills shoved beneath our door at ungodly hours, only a quiet lobby area overseen by a smiling young Austrian lady, with tea- and coffee-making facilities, and a generous supply of alcohol to be paid for via an honesty box when no member of staff was available.

Such an example of trust is rarely seen back home.

After an unexpectedly sound sleep and a quick breakfast in a neighbourhood bakery, we spent the first day wandering the broad *Straßen*, each one seemingly deeper and wider than the last, the clean light stone of the ornate apartment blocks standing stoic against a sky pregnant with tomorrow's snow creating the impression of canyons carved from grey granite, syenite and marble. Our necks ached from looking up at buildings as our feet crunched over pavement frost that glimmered like quartz dust and the grit salt granules that seared holes in the surface patina of glimmering white.

Ice droplets decorated the lamp posts and the sun was a monochrome watercolour painting hung on the wall of the sky.

'Everything is so crisp,' I murmured so quietly that no one could possibly have heard it. 'Everything is so *clean.*'

As we wandered the streets, I breathed in the city's many scents. When I exhaled I imagined a thick plume of black smoke that represented the anxiety I had been carrying around within me. Up and away it went, dissipating in the stiff air. I was attempting to let negative feelings go and banish the tensions and occasional flashes of terror that had underpinned an exhausting year.

I had recently submitted a novel, the first to my new publisher, and now I was a spent husk, a walking cadaver with pieces of coal for eyes, the last reserves of my psychic energies having been poured into a final edit. I had been in one of my 'states' and, as is so often the case, it had taken all my willpower to get myself vertical and dressed, and to leave the house in order to get to the airport in time. The novel was just one of the reasons for the tension and terrors; the others were more nebulous and not as easily identifiable.

As has happened before, the airport had represented, to my frazzled mind at least, a kind of slaughterhouse of the near future, an existential cattle shed from which my natural inclination was to turn and flee. It was the people everywhere that did it for me, all of them in a hyperstate of pre-flight excitement that changed the energy of the place and singed the edges of my already fragile senses. I had spent so much time alone of late that the sight of all those people flowing around me, their bodies occasionally brushing mine, their voices too loud and their breath sometimes smelling of scented vape smoke and morning lager, did not help my mental state. Everything seemed too loud, too bright.

I vomited in the toilets.

But we were here now and I could smell the warm salty hum of blinkered horses, their tails plaited, fetlocks decorated and steam rising from their flanks. Their drivers idled in the carriages behind them, awaiting the next wave of tourists to take around the city.

Other scents intermingled to form a collective perfume of old Europe. In the Christmas market the hiss and sizzle of bratwursts on street vendors' griddles overlapped with the cinnamon of warm strudel and the spices of mulled wine, while simmering pots of goulash, deep-fried doughnuts and strong coffee stirred the appetite.

Across broad *Plätze* and down other *Straßen*, other smells: vanilla pods, waffle sugar, roast chestnuts, dark chocolate, cigarette smoke – even the most ardently committed reformed smoker still occasionally feels the lure of tobacco on a sub-zero day – schnitzel, car fumes, hot oil. More pretzels.

We wore clothing that was too warm even for northern England in December: our most expensive coats, plus scarves, gloves and hats, and our best leather shoes.

There is something about European capital cities in winter that makes one want to parade. Perhaps the need to move and look and observe and breathe is a form of time travel. This was certainly recognised and enjoyed by the French *flâneurs* of the nineteenth century, whose constant strolling and deliberate act of looking was considered an art form in itself. That we pompously opted to do something similar while wearing our best coats and shoes only seemed to draw us closer to those wanderers who had gone before, and in those moments – at the turn of a new corner, peeking down an obscure alley – the decades and centuries (and language barriers) slipped away as we fell into step with our European ancestors, the soles of the centuries tapping the hard pavements in unison.

We are three. Bernt, Elrick and me.

A devil's dozen hounds we have with us; two are out on their maiden pursuit, their first winter.

Now and again we have to cleave away the snow that becomes impacted in the paws of these two with a branch or twig so that it does not freeze and make them lame. When that is done they bound back to the pack, pink tongues unfurled and dangling like cut hide strips hanging at the tannery. Often along the trail they disappear from sight, sinking deep in the drifts, but we do not stop to dig them out. This they must learn themselves, lest they become lazy or are turned out into the woods forever and must survive the season alone.

Mainly we move as one, the pack a shifting shape with the same two elder dogs heading the chase. Vop, usually, or Yeff. Both are still lean and strong, long-rested and ready after a hot slothful summer and mild autumn past.

The others follow their lead, and we follow them. Bernt to the left side, Elrick to the right, and me minding the rear for laggers, or the sight of any cunning hart, boar, wolf or fox that dares to think he is smart enough to circle back on us for a second look.

That evening we went to the Secession gallery, where Ed Ruscha was exhibiting a collection of paintings of American flags and drum skins on which were written phrases from Mark Twain's *Pudd'nhead Wilson*. The works were shown in a white concrete box of a room that echoed with the staccato chatter of German students. We didn't stay long.

Downstairs in the climate-controlled underground gallery Gustav Klimt's *Beethoven Frieze* of 1902 glittered golden; the swirls, snaking patterns and saggy dugs of the naked women who, according to the gallery notes, represented Lasciviousness, Wantonness and Intemperance, seemed alive. High up on the wall on which they had been directly painted they appeared to writhe coquettishly, as outside night fell on the eve of the winter solstice.

Looking at the frieze, I was surprised to find that I felt very little except a bout of heartburn caused by all the pastry I had eaten over the course of the day; I had left my bottle of Gaviscon back in our room, and was more focused on the acid reflux silently blazing beneath my sternum than the once-controversial 'hostile forces' of Klimt's lewd figures. I wished my critical faculties could have been more astute, but sometimes the vessel that carries the mind rebels in a way that is difficult to ignore.

The Viennese we found to be rather brusque in temperament. Though far from hostile, they were frequently terse in their manner, especially those working in the service industry or of an older generation. Several times in cafes and restaurants our smiles or attempts at small talk were met by withering eyerolls or, worse, blank faces. When I asked for the bill in a traditional tea room whose customers seemed to be comprised of doddery old dears slowly spooning soup into their quivering mouths, and whose windows were so completely covered with steam that the busy street outside was hidden from view, the waiter offered little but the tiniest irritable twitch of one bushy eyebrow in recognition of my request. The sausages were well seasoned, though, and came with a delicious side order of grated horseradish, so we took the moral high ground and tipped generously anyway.

Not for the inhabitants of Austria's capital the endearingly droll and often misunderstood humour of their neighbours in Germany either. Though the city had recently polled as the number-one capital in the world in terms of living standards, many of its elder residents whom we encountered didn't seem to be outwardly happy. But perhaps we were projecting too high an expectation upon them, and not giving enough credence to cultural differences.

For some reason these dining hall observations made me think about the Vienna-set novel that I had read recently, about the rise of fascism and how such regimes only gain strength because of the complicity of those occupying the upper echelons of society. Right-wing ideologies were now gathering traction across Europe once more, and surely needed to be nipped in the bud before their roots were allowed to bed in further. The problem was, many of the fascists were now disguising themselves as everyday concerned citizens, their masks of old swapped for the comfort and safety of a social media avatar or a shared conspiracy that had been allowed to blossom unchallenged.

That I got all this from watching a dozen or so Viennese pensioners tuck into their veal and *Sachertorte* is perhaps as damning an indictment of my own state of mind as anything else.

Either way, none of it was helping my anxiety, which bubbled deep within me, a tar pit in my stomach.

Those who we did find to be friendly seemed to be either in their twenties and in possession of a positive energy and sense of openness that was lacking in their elder counterparts, which gave me a glimmer of hope for the future, or they invariably came from further afield – Berlin, Italy or Japan.

Vienna is the perfect city for temporary time travel, yet the mundanity of the modern world is never far away. That morning as we dressed I had turned on the BBC World Service and listened to the rolling news broadcast quietly in the background. According to a report, all flights at Gatwick were delayed due to the sighting of a suspected drone or drones near the airport. *Travel chaos* was the phrase they used, as they always do. A reporter said these words as he stood outside, shivering in the cold, the airport so far behind him that it was reduced to little but a grey shape in the distance. It could have been a battleship or a shopping centre or an ancient forest. Perhaps it was.

The trudge and the stumble through great expanses of nothingness. The long unbroken spells of stopping and looking, hours from anywhere.

The watching and waiting. Tracking and stalking.

Then suddenly a blur of fur.

A streak of hot pelt moving at great speed like a spear flung deep into the pounding heart of winter. The dogs are focused so totally that the only thought is their quarry, the scent so strong as to send them into a frenzied state. Tails up, noses down, they scour the ground, divining it for answers, for secrets, for flesh.

Perhaps they smell boar, the best bounty there is. Perhaps we think we smell it too, wishing it into being, sizzling and popping over hot coals in the dreams of tomorrow, the three of us meat-drunk on the very thought and the smiles of our children, their cheeks flushed with the glow of satisfaction. We're already picturing the quiet glances of pride worn by our women through the darkest December days.

But it does not do to dream in the daytime.

It does not do to stray from the path.

Confused, the dogs scatter.

The moment passes.

It, like the creature, is gone.

That night, feeling bloated from the evening meal – charred calamari, seabass, something involving chickpeas – we headed back to the hotel room to take our trousers off and stretch out on the mattress beneath the Magritte lampshades.

I flicked through the TV channels and happened on a Syrian news show broadcasting grainy footage of tanks being fired at by rocket launchers, interspersed with shots of men waving and then discharging Kalashnikovs over their heads while dancing raucously to music.

I called my wife over and we watched it together, the changing colours from the TV screen continually altering the ambience of our darkened room.

Some of the men were wearing the same insulated Puffa jackets that small-time drug dealers wore in cold English towns in the 1990s. These scenes were played on a loop, explosion after explosion, the triumphant volleys of gunshots becoming louder and more frenzied, the music pulsating, slightly off-key so as to disorientate. No women featured in the clips. We tried to laugh at the absurdity of this display of machismo and pornographic violence that constituted the state news channel, but any attempt at humour felt hollow. We both knew that there were more than likely men in the tanks being blown up, that this wasn't just for show.

The relentless music was dizzying and the tar pit of anxiety bubbled within me again. I had to turn over.

The room felt too hot. I fiddled with the radiator settings.

A film channel offered a selection of movies, few of which either of us were interested in, and we clicked through until we settled on *Phantom Thread*. I've always enjoyed the work of Daniel Day-Lewis. I first saw him when I was around ten years old in his breakthrough role in *My Beautiful Laundrette*, and then in *My Left Foot* and *In the Name of the Father*, and later when he starred in such big-hitters as *There Will Be Blood*.

There is also the story of Day-Lewis quitting acting for a while to become a cobbler in Italy, a tale perhaps circulated in order to fuel the mythology of him as one of the most enigmatic actors of his time. Or perhaps he just genuinely wanted to make some shoes; after all, people may not always want films in their lives, but they will almost certainly always need shoes.

Phantom Thread was his first movie in five years and his last before his retirement, so we settled back to watch it.

It is perhaps most memorable for an early scene in which Day-Lewis's English couturier Reynolds Woodcock, resplendent in a cravat and speaking in a distinctly mannered, almost simpering, voice through-out, orders a lavish and indulgent breakfast.

I happened to know that this section had been shot in a small hotel in the North Yorkshire village of Robin Hood's Bay, the location for the novel I had recently finished writing and which was the source of my exhaustion and anxiety, though for some reason I was more tickled by Day-Lewis's delivery of the concluding words of his breakfast request: '. . . and some sausages'.

We laughed at that line a lot, my wife and I, and over the next few days I found myself repeating the phrase frequently, both internally and out loud too, often when

I least expected it, occasionally surprising myself and anyone in close proximity who happened to hear me.

After the film ended we both slept, the phrase '. . . and some sausages' echoing in my subconscious like a rubber ball being thwacked around a squash court. Over the coming days the mantra began to take on an almost malevolent quality as it embedded itself in my head, an unwanted squatter in the chatter of my every waking moment.

———————

Pink is the snow as we enter deep forest as silent and still as a church of wattle. The trees are wind-bent spires. A hallowed place, sometimes a man can find God here. Sometimes he finds himself instead. Other times, nothing at all. A nothingness so deep and diabolical he must stuff a cold clenched fist into his mouth to stop the screaming. It consumes us. It consumes us all.

———————

The main reason for our extended pre-Christmas break in this old city was to view the exhibition of paintings, drawings and prints by Pieter Bruegel the Elder that had been assembled by the Kunsthistorisches Museum. I had long been a fan of the Dutch master's depictions of sixteenth-century rural landscapes and peasant life, and was particularly excited at the opportunity to view his most famous work, *The Hunters in the Snow*, at close quarters.

So, it seemed, was a substantial fraction of the population of mainland Europe, for the three-month exhibition had long since sold out. Bruegel's works were so old and fragile that they rarely travelled, so this 'summit of masterpieces', as the museum was billing it, was a rare occasion reflected in the exhibition's title: *Once In A Lifetime*.

My wife and I had discovered that tickets were unavailable a week earlier, and I had emailed the museum's publicist in advance of our visit to explain that I was a writer and sometime journalist who was visiting the city, and that I hoped to write a short story entitled '*The Hunters in the Snow*' for a forthcoming collection. It was at best a semi-truth, a hastily drawn offhand request that I only half-heartedly intended to honour, if at all, yet years of journalistic experience had at least taught me that shy children get no sweets, and that wanton blagging is an art form that requires confidence, a certain minimal knowledge of the subject and, I'm ashamed to admit, a faint air of entitlement when faced with obstacles that might turn other people away.

The day before we flew out, a response had arrived from the museum's publicist confirming that I had received press accreditation for myself and a guest.

Before we left the hotel, the BBC World Service offered an update on the Gatwick story. A newsreader said that flights in and out of the airport were temporarily suspended while police and airport authorities tried to ascertain whether the reported sightings of the drones were to be deemed a real threat. They were treating it as a possible terrorist incident and undertaking enquiries in the local area. Footage showed huge queues of people, some of them carrying skis, and a departure board with the words *DELAYED* or *CANCELLED* flashing beside every scheduled flight.

We arrived at the Kunsthistorisches Museum to see a throng of people outside.

In the main atrium the excited voices of hundreds, perhaps thousands, of visitors echoed around the great chamber as they had their bags searched, checked in their coats and donned headsets that provided a running commentary, but which I always eschew in such circumstances, reasoning, perhaps arrogantly, that I prefer to arrive at my own interpretations of the work.

Our names didn't appear to be on the press list at the main entrance, but such was the confident manner in which we presented ourselves, and so harried were those at the ticket office, that they waved us right on through and up the twin staircases, where we repeated the process at the next security check. Once again they couldn't find our names, but I presented a printout of the email received from the museum's publicist and we were allowed to continue. The crowd thickened as we approached the final security check – again no name, again we talked our way through – and then we were in amongst the detailed dioramas of sixteenth-century Low Countries life.

It was busy, and warm too. I took off my scarf, rolled it up and shoved it into my pocket alongside my hat and fingerless gloves. As I unbuttoned my coat I immediately wished I had brought a bottle of water.

The thing I noticed first was not the art itself, or the people vying for a position to see it, but the sound of the creaking parquet floor under the weight of hundreds of pairs of shifting feet. It had a timbre and a rhythm to it that seemed entirely detached from the room, yet was so clearly a part of it. I stood for a minute or two just listening to the floor and feeling claustrophobic, before allowing myself to be drawn along with the crowd past the early pencil sketches of landscapes and into a room that held the subject of my fascination. There it was: *The Hunters in the Snow* (1565).

———

Ghosted from view, the beast is unseen. Light prints of toes pressed into snow disappear amongst the trail mess of dogs that have crossed one another in the pursuit. Was it even a boar? We reach a stream and the scent goes as cold as the water that I stoop to sip and pad at my throbbing temples. The dogs turn circles, two niggle and scrap, and I whistle to Elrick, who whistles to Bernt, the three of us holding the line. Around us the forest groans. Black timber looms. Wet feet.

No birds.

———

You probably know the painting yourself, even if the title is not familiar.

The work's importance lies not merely in its survival as an artefact of its time – but in the fact that it tells us as much as a hundred thousand written words possibly could.

At least two dozen people of different nationalities stood around *The Hunters in the Snow*, my view of it blocked by bodies radiating a collective energy that was discernible as a low hum. I angled for a view, my exhibition programme in hand. My coat felt a little damp, and I clammy beneath it. I tugged at the collar of my jumper. The polished wooden tiles of the parquet floor continued to creak underfoot.

Around the room, similar clusters of people were vying for space near Bruegel's more recognisable paintings. People would periodically break away from these cliques and move to another one, drawn by the opportunity to document the experience with a selfie. Everyone was part of the same swarm that was moving through the rooms, an ever-pulsing mass, absorbing, documenting, then moving on.

I turned back to *The Hunters in the Snow*. I now found myself in one of these clusters, akin to a mosh pit at a punk gig, a ritual based upon certain unspoken agreed-upon rules refined over several decades.

If that was the case, and I was a willing participant in the mosh pit, then the subject of our attention – the spark that lit our tinder, as it were – was not a band of musicians expressing themselves through the medium of electricity, but the work of a solitary painter. Here we were, jostling with pointed elbows, phones raised and tilted, feeling one another's breaths down our necks, snapping photographs and uploading them via satellite technology to social media, all for a snowy scene created by a man who died five years after the birth of William Shakespeare.

This thought was a revelation. Here was someone who had us under a spell, someone who in this very moment – and the next, and the next, perhaps for evermore – was reaching forward into a future world he could never have possibly conceived, even with the most fertile of imaginations.

———

Snagged on brambles: a twist of fur the colour of Bernt's beard. I press it to his flushed face and we stand in silence for a moment and then turn in the direction of the low-lying tunnel through the scrub. It's a run carved by a fox, for sure; a fine pursuit for a pelt but little else, foxes being

*bad for the eating. Too bitter. On another day it might be a
good game for the dogs but our stores are low and the winter
is long and this is not a game.*

———

It took what seemed like an inordinately long time to
get into a position to view the painting without obstruc-
tion. I noticed that the museum was relaxed about the
way in which we were all free to wander and get close to
the works, much more so than the galleries in London.
I didn't notice any security guards pacing the rooms or
yawning, bored on a chair in the corner. It was refresh-
ingly trusting.

The gallery did, however, prevent us from bringing
bags upstairs and by this point I was thirsty and thinking about water often. I'm not good when I'm thirsty.
It's the same when I'm hungry. I get irritable, distracted.
My thoughts move sideways and splinter. My limbs
become leaden, and my skin prickles with heat. Anxiety
writhes in my stomach too, as it did now. A sour snake
crawled up through my chest and into my gullet. Soon
it would be at my throat.

To distract myself from the catastrophising that was
threatening to take over my mind, and to escape these
negative thoughts, I found myself checking my phone:
the Gatwick drone story was still ongoing. A report from
mid-morning said that all flights had been cancelled.
Travellers were irate, confused and tired. Many people

were going away for Christmas, or travelling home, and had no idea what was happening. Others had missed their connections and were now stretched out across chairs or lying on floors using their hand luggage as pillows, with T-shirts, scarves or hats pulled down across their eyes. The news reporter interviewed some of those who were awake. There were Mexicans and Poles and Australians and English. No one knew who the owners of the drones were, and furthermore no one was able to say who exactly had seen them, or indeed where and when. Many of the travellers were hungry and thirsty.

It was the wrong story to read in such a situation, as I now felt my heart thumping in my chest; I licked my dry lips and swallowed once, then twice.

When I looked up I found that I was very close to *The Hunters in the Snow* and there was no way I was going to relinquish this spot in order to walk back through several rooms and down the sweeping marble staircase and into the basement toilets, all for some water.

A cooling mint might have helped my thirst and I cursed for not being equipped with any, as I've always prided myself on being the person who has the aspirin, a pen, the mints, a paperclip, a comb. Whatever you need, I've got it. I even carry a spare Ventolin inhaler, though I'm not asthmatic.

At last I was in front of the painting, as close to it as I could be, front and centre, and the next thing I knew, I was in it. Breathing its still air and feeling the crunch of crusted snow underfoot, the pulse of my heart in my temples and wrists. I was looking out across the landscape, over the roofs of the houses and the bridge to the frozen ponds where the people of the village – my village – were skating, and the boughs of the winter trees were creaking, their spindly branches rattling, the sap frozen, black crows circling overhead, and in the distance mist was settling on the great rocky scarps that poked upwards, jutting accusations against the sky.

My numb fingers curled around the long spear whose point was untainted by big game blood and I used it to steady myself through the final deep drifts before we split our formation, each turning towards home, in no hurry now, for the empty-handed hunter is never in a rush to return. My legs were soaked, limbs leaden. I was bone-cold and nearly beaten by the day.

And there were the smells that drifted across the plain: woodsmoke from the fire where a pot was already boiling, ready to take the hair off a beast we had not caught. Somewhere unseen, broth. All around, decay, damp and midden stench too.

I was right there, breathing the lowlands air, my muscles aching from the futile chase of nothingness. And it was all so beautiful, it was all so right.

And it was all too much.

The warmth and the crowds and the need for water were becoming overwhelming. This was not good. No. This was not good at all. With one foot in each era, in each world, I felt as if I were being torn asunder from somewhere deep inside. I was here and there, then and now, past and present, hot and cold, thirsty and hungry, exhilarated and anxious, exhausted and enlivened, all at the same time.

The room was taking on strange new dimensions, a contortion of curved lines and fisheye perspectives.

And where was my wife?

A long time had passed since I had last seen her. I checked my phone to see if she had texted but all I got was a BBC News update that flights were still grounded and the police were no closer to finding out who had flown drones into the airspace. The words swirled before me. Why was no one here screaming? They all seemed so excited or happy or deep in conversation or preoccupied with their phones and their headsets. In the face of such beauty, why weren't they running into the street, naked, jumping on parked cars? Overwhelmed by the existential horror of time and the turning of the planet, life and death, and the whole of it, why weren't they pulling off windscreen wipers and hurling their own faeces and smashing their heads into the mirrored glass windows of the great shining buildings of this city, and all cities?

How could they hold it all together?

My head and stomach are empty jugs and my legs tremble. Food is all I think about as we trudge the hill and I see the watermill, the ponds. I know that Bernt and Elrick will be feeling the same and if they are not thinking of food then they are thinking about the shame of empty hands returning to the village. In the eyes of our people we are failures.

Today we are lesser men.

———

I'm found on the gallery floor, out cold. Several people are leaning over me and speaking in German. They all wear a look of concern, which I find highly embarrassing. Someone passes me a bottle of water, another helps me sit up. The tiled parquet floor is creaking around me.

When I stand, my head and stomach are empty jugs and my legs tremble. My feet and legs are soaked up to the knees, but I can't understand why. I'm still clutching my coat. I assure everyone that I am alright by forcing a smile and giving them a thumbs up, which just seems absurd given the location and the situation. I take a seat and they gradually drift away, one or two of them looking back at me, conferring, then carrying on into the next room.

I take out my phone to find out where my wife is. The Gatwick story has reached a conclusion. Flights are now scheduled for take-off, though the huge backlog still means that there's a great deal of confusion amongst travellers about when they might get to finally leave the airport and continue their onward journeys. Police have found no drones, or owners of drones. Maybe there were no drones at all.

It is a late morning on a cold winter Thursday in the heart of Europe in the twenty-first century when a message arrives from my wife: *Where are you??*

I reply: *Been hunting. Lunch?*

Old Ginger

Mind Old Ginger the gamekeeper. Myths abound where he's concerned.

Famous through the Border country, was Old Ginger; a legend to some, a purpling, heather-lurking menace to many more.

Pheasants and pleasant folk stopping in their weekend homes feared him equally, as well they should have, for the wee man wasn't entirely right. Too long on the moors alone with his traps had turned him. Sent his head west, they said.

The man at the big house kept him on, though. He gave Old Ginger free rein and a good run of the estate, by all accounts. A job for life. So long as the birds were ripe for shooting come August when the red-faced brokers came yodelling through in search of fur, feather and fin, he kept the old boy in his employ. Left him to it.

More than that, Old Ginger had worked for the man at the big house's daddy, and his daddy had worked for his daddy before him, so sticking to the traditional ways of the laird and his gamekeeper ensured the old order was kept alive. Preserving continuity when all else on the island was in flux was important then. Still is, to some.

Only the man at the big house wasn't a laird as he liked to pretend: he had made his money first through inheritance and latterly by selling knock-down sports clobber through a pile-'em-high retail chain famed for its illegitimate working practices; he wouldn't have known a title of the realm if it was pinned to his left nut by the Queen herself. And Old Ginger was less a game-keeper and more of a sadist with a cudgel and a growing grudge against yomping outsiders.

But still, the bossman had a family crest drawn up, and staff from down the town, and different cars for different days, and shooting parties that meant he could play the plastic laird, so he kept Old Ginger on, filling the feeders with grain, eyeballing the pine plantations and scouring the moors for prey of either the animal or the human variety.

See, that was Old Ginger's problem. Decades up here had him so entrenched in the landscape that he'd lost his ability to differentiate between man and beast; all was quarry for Ginger. His was a world of blood and snares, raptors and hares. His architecture was bog-bone and feather. Wind and rain. Grass and heather.

Blade and gullet. Gun and bullet.

It was his way or the straight-as-an arrow tarmac highway that the Romans had cut through the red upland sod two thousand years ago, the moors his fiefdom and pity any poor bastard in a rustling cagoule that crossed it unawares.

You heard so many stories about Ginger that you just knew some of them had to be true, such as the one about him leaping out on lone folk and battering them senseless. Or the dogs he kept in cages and fed with a special mash dosed with speed to keep them tightly wound and radge for ratting round the grain feeders or, most likely, to drive away any nosy cunt that might be nebbing round his sad stone box of a house up on the moor edge.

They said he had had a wife once, but she couldn't hack it. Got sick of the magistrates' court, the freezer full of animal parts and the blood under his nails as he pawed at her with his big fingers. Pelts in the airing cupboard. Offal in the pantry.

You'd know Ginger's face if you'd ever clocked him: wind-worn and a head half bald, the rest of it crowned by a frayed red mane. Cod-eyed too, was Ginger. One eyeball forever wandering to a place inside his little skull. Mind, he was short too. You'll find that most moor men of a certain bloodline are. The best ones, anyway. They say the tall lads blow over like firs in a gale, but the stout boys just lean into it and plough on through. Legs like hams, had Old Ginger. The same circumference all the way down, they were shaped by the hills and made for walking, though his knees were shot from a lifetime of stumbling through rut and runnel, so in those later years he took to riding roughshod on a quad bike instead.

And then there was his uniform, unchanged as long as anyone had known him: steel-toed boots and the same fingerless gloves. No coat for him either, just layer upon layer of shirt and jumper, a few of each, all matted and wadded together into a fleecy shell of sweat and dirt and wool that he was said to sleep in, upright in his living room chair, banked fire glowing, logs popping.

Pity anyone who tried to lift a brace of pheasant or snag a few hares from the estate with Old Ginger about. Broken bones were their reward and that was not the worst of it. One lad he tied up in the top wood and humiliated with pine cones in ways that don't bear repeating.

Pity the creatures of tooth and claw even more, though. Because Old Ginger had traps and snares set up well away from any prying eyes, a mile or two's walk from any road or track, all the way up top, tucked into a fold of the moor or buried in a copse. Lagged to a stone wall, shoved into a stump. He was always trying out new methods and updating old techniques for the sheer thrill of it. Once, in cold vengeance against a fox that had been seen one too many times skulking the grounds with a pheasant in its mouth, he took a small piece of sprung steel and tied it up with some dissolvable catgut cord. Then he boiled up some meat parts with special herbs to attract the creature, and he shaped it into a fat ball around the steel and set it in a spot it was known to pass on its dawn rounds. The fox was not seen again, sure to have died a slow and diabolical death somewhere, all cut up from the trap that snapped deep in the poor thing's stomach.

And then there were Old Ginger's cages: great big things, maybe six feet tall and fifteen feet across. Birds of prey were his target – the raptors that fed on the big man's grouse and pheasant. Old Ginger wouldn't stand for that. If the foxes hadn't got at the eggs and they somehow made it through hatching, then it was likely they could end up snatched away skywards when they were still defenceless balls of down, so the gamekeeper liked to strike first, with no quarter.

His cages had trapped hen harriers and peregrines. Buzzards, kestrels and sparrowhawks aplenty too. Enough owls to stuff a mattress. Red kites were especially fine catches, but you had to be careful because they'd been wing-tagged following reintroduction a few years back and even possessing the bones of a stripped red kite could spell time inside.

Only once had he snared himself a golden eagle, its wingspan greater than the height of him, its beak like a sharpened shank. Talons like something from mythology. He dreamed of it for months afterwards. It haunted his sleep.

And here's the worst bit. Old Ginger's preferred method was to live-bait the traps with crows, mainly.

But a trapped blue-black bird wasn't enough of a lure for him. No. He would get himself a crow or blackbird or any hoodlum nesting in the estate's wide-ranging woodlands, and then he would heat a spike in the pit of a fire and press it into that poor thing's eyes. First one, then the other. Blinded it. And the crow would be screeching and squirming, but Old Ginger just bound its beak with an elastic band and gripped it tighter until the job was done.

Then he put it into the cage and left it there, and the bird would think it had died and gone to the next world, but a world where a cruel wind still blows in across the moor, whatever the season. There was a gap at the top of the cage, you see, and the raptor would clock the crow, swoop down, and then find itself stuck like a lobster in a Craster creel, too daft or disorientated to seek a way out. And then it was his: ownership passed from branch and eyrie and sky to Old Ginger. In his hands lay the bird's fate.

Old Ginger never took a drink. He never went down the town to sink a few with the boys, and that was his downfall. Because the boys will always turn a blind eye to a transgression and look after their own. They're tight like that. Passing time and country tradition has made them that way. Ginger claimed he didn't like the taste, but it was people that bothered him. Being around them, trapped in rooms with them. Their conversation. Their laughter. Still, maybe if he had taken a drink, he wouldn't have crossed swords with Young Kipper.

Now, Young Kipper ran a tight team of game boys. Poachers to a man. They did it for the sport, for the challenge, for the same reason their fathers' fathers had. Hares, rabbits, pheasants, grouse – it didn't matter what. Foxes and badgers. The occasional deer. Because they too liked to keep the old ways alive, to try out the techniques their grandads had taught them as soon as they could walk: the slipknots, the big lamp, the long net and all of that. They were grafters, Kipper's crew. Workers by day and poachers by night. They sold their beasts on the sly to the outdoor markets or to butchers in far-flung towns, or else they kept what they caught for their own pots.

One was known to cook up a rabbit cassoulet good enough to serve in a Parisian restaurant.

And where Old Ginger was cruel, Young Kipper was mad. Next-level mad. The old boy never caught him at it but he knew what Kip's boys were up to, and it galled him to see this new generation filching his best birds. Only once did he confront him, out on the moor, one on one, but the younger man just laughed and cited his right to roam and that was that. No square go, just festering resentment.

So the gamekeeper took revenge. He plotted until he found a weak spot to exploit. Young Kipper had two ravens. Beautiful things. He'd raised them since day one, turned them into pets. He'd been on the telly with them; he was damn near famous for his ravens, was

Young Kipper. Well, naturally, Old Ginger had to have one of them.

And that's exactly what he did, snatching it at night, though no one ever knew how, for Kipper kept them locked up good in his long garden at the end of town, so it seemed Old Ginger was the greatest gamekeeper turned poacher of the lot of them.

Not long after Kipper found one of his beloved ravens vanished, a night raid on Old Ginger's cages solved the mystery when it was found dead and blinded. Live bait gone wrong. He was inconsolable, and all of his boys knew this could only end one way. Retribution was as inevitable as the turning of the leaves. Calculated resolve took over; Young Kipper left it a week or two, then went out alone. He stalked the stalker. Put in the hours.

It was in the gloaming of an October evening, when Ginger's back was turned, that Young Kipper pounced, bundling him into one of Ginger's own baited cages up beyond the reservoir, the most remote one there was. In that cage Young Kipper pulled out some pruning shears that he had sharpened up good with stone and oil, and he took a few bits of Old Ginger back for his remaining raven. An eyelid. A fingertip.

An earlobe. A lower lip.

He put them in his pocket and then he left the cage and walked out across the moor with only the waxy light of a hunter's moon to guide him.

Old Ginger made it back, just about, minus a few vitals. Six stints of surgery sorted some of the physical aspects, but by then his mind had gone, part of him forever in that cage: the blood from an eye and a hand and an ear and a mouth pooling in the blackening night, bird shit and feathers coating him as he writhed in the dirt, reaching out into the darkness.

An Act of Erasure

It was September, that month when the scent of smoke on the breeze signals the coming season of decay. The trees become suspended with skeletons and the writhing worms turn the soil below.

My grandad had been unwell for some time.

He had recently sold the grocer's shop above which he and my gran had lived for all of their married life, nearly half a century, and moved into an end-terrace. One day he returned home with his brown trousers soaked to the waist.

'You're wet through, you daft beggar,' said my gran, noticing that he would not meet her eye as he stripped down to his thin white bones.

It transpired that he had waded out into the slate soup of the North Sea, but something had made him turn back.

She kept finding a hammer in different parts of the house: in the bathroom, the kitchen, beneath the bed.

When she asked him what it was for, Grandad admitted that he had intended to use it on himself. In his troubled state, there was a logic to keeping a means of destruction close to hand.

Then one morning when Gran popped to the corner shop to buy a newspaper and bacon, he tied a rope around his neck and jumped from the stairs, and for one still moment the noise of his life was silenced.

When she returned she found his false teeth down on the carpet, beneath his swaying shadow.

After the funeral and the flowers, the buffet and the visitors, after the obituary and the sedatives, but long before the nightmares faded into manageable nocturnal shapes, one day while tidying up my gran found in a drawer several tubes of denture glue, all of them unopened.

The Bloody Bell

With the wind at our backs we walked the wall.

It was a whistling wind, one that shrieked like wild woodland creatures torn apart in the deepest pits of our childhood nightmares one moment, dropping to a low sonorous drone the next. Here the wind became hypnotic and malevolent, as if the stones themselves were groaning with pain as the bevelled-bladed breeze whipped at our cloaks, uncoiled our rags and tipped our hats tumbling away before us like mad birds.

Even when we huddled into the short shadows of the raised bank along which the great stone serpent structure slithered off into the fog or hunkered low into the vallum ditch, the wind would not abate. Instead it toyed with us by changing direction and spitting like a cornered wildcat the first swirling whorl of snowflakes in our faces.

There was a fury to its darkening mood, a foreshadowing of the journey to come.

We had been but one night and two days out and already time was twisting and spiralling so that the low silver winter sun shifted across the sky in the blink of an eye, yet at other times mere moments could appear endless.

A sun that gave off no heat.

A sun that offered no solace.

It was a shimmering thing of beauty, like cooling mercury pooled in the dub of a smelter's furnace floor, yet useless except to guide us east from the shifting sands of Solway through the Eden Valley to where it was said this wall ended and the salt of another sea stung the nostrils and a man of great wealth awaited us.

Our party numbered six.

There was Colly the Bellman, whose every other spoken word came with a rattling cough that sounded like Death himself was shaking tarn pebbles in his fist, and his apprentice Foul Wendle, whose breath was as rotten as a rat that's been found drowned belly-up in the midden runnel.

This sackless pair carried with them a great bronze bell that Colly had spent a year casting and polishing and buffing and tuning, and it was as big as I am tall, which is to say not that tall, but as heavy as four fattened sheep when strapped to the handcart that they took in turns to drag and push as far as the wall would take them.

This bell was the reason for our journey as it was my father who was charged with guiding coughing Colly and Foul Wendle, and to ensure that no hands but theirs were laid upon it all the way from one briny water to the next, for it was deemed more valuable than most men's lives, and Fath had quite a name for fighting. No person of any colour, tongue or standing had licked him yet because when the fury was rising in him Fath was one of the most feared beasts of the northlands. Men of the emperor's wall had given money, malt mash and meat to watch him, a mere man of poor Carvetii blood – someone who had sailed no seas and joined no army – fight their best soldier until only one was left standing. And it was never a wall man.

'Like the wall stones in the breeze, I bend to no one,' he said loud and often.

We brought with us our Peg, my sister, for Mother was not long in the sod and a girl of her age could not be left alone at the hearth of the homestead, for to do that would be to tie a doe in the clearing of a copse that you know echoes to the sound of wolves who have its scent in their shining snouts. No, Peg could not tarry, even if she was the only daughter of feared Fath, for some men would sooner strike first and think on their actions later.

Then there was the Priest Popple, who walked to spread the word of Jesu, who he reckoned to be quite the man of magic and miracles, though we all knew that the priest was fond of the ferment so prone to riddle-spinning. A pious man never known to have creased his face with laughter, he carried with him two pieces of timber lagged crossways and laid across his shoulder, a most pointless and burdensome piece of kit that Colly the Bellman said was green but still keen for burning, but he got a clump from the Priest Popple when he tried to do as much.

And then there was me, with a slingshot and the sharpest eye, bagging rabbits and keeping watch. The bell's clapper I was also given to carry across my back by Colly, who said it was a special honour to bear such a thing, though the aches and blisters and welts it gave me suggested both he and Wendle were too lazy to take it themselves.

'This clapper is heavy,' I said.

Colly replied by coughing until he was near blue.

'That's as may be,' he said. 'But cherish your aches, young lad, for what use is a bell without a clapper?'

'He's right,' said the Priest Popple. 'Your burden is holy.'

At this I saw Foul Wendle smirking.

'Come,' said Fath. 'The storm is set to rage. We'll seek a hollow somewhere to fetch up.'

———

We awoke to thick snow and the sound of Foul Wendle moaning most absurdly.

Fath stuck his head out the slit of our leather tent and there was Wendle shirtless, the snow blowing around him.

'It's my master, Colly,' he said, then added 'Colly the Bellman', as if there were any other.

'Well, what about him?'

'His face is a mask.'

'A mask,' said Fath.

'He is dead.'

'Are you sure?'

'His lips are the shape of an eternal cough and his limbs as stiff as that clapper that your boy carries,' said Wendle. 'I reckon it's this bell what's seen him done for. It's cursed.'

'What rot you talk,' said Fath. 'Colly drinks goose fat by the tankard and lies at night with any pox-scarred harlot from Whitehaven to the Wall's End that his Roman bit will buy him. He was bound to sleep with his feet up one of these days.'

At this the Priest Popple appeared from his tent.

'What's this stink?'

'You'll have to help with the bell cart,' said Fath. 'Colly's carked it.'

'But I have the cross of Jesu to carry.'

'That's tough tagnuts for you, then.'

The Priest Popple spat in the snow. He looked at the bell. 'It's ungainly.'

'But I thought you said all burdens are holy,' I piped.

Fath laughed at this.

'Come on, holy man. We'll put the bellman in the ditch where he'll be on ice till spring and then the ravens can be at him. Let's get to moving before this storm fills our bones.'

We pushed through boscage thicket spiked with hoar frost and tussocks of brittle spinney. It was our third day and the going was slow. My feet were numb, the clapper heavy on my back.

We walked with the wall to our left. Beyond it masses of whinstone pushed up from the earth in great columns around which a gust could blow a slight boy right off the edge.

Worse still were those who lived out there. It was said that these roughhouses had been making gains on the empire forts and that some had fallen to them. Word said that the soldiers of Rome had been called away by whoever it was that did the calling, and they had gone to fight in foreign fields, leaving their stores ripe for plundering by these fearsome Caledonians.

We Carvetii boys were alright, though. We Carvetii boys of the Solway Plain, who chiselled our names or rosette markings in milestones across the Land of Cumber, had been trading with the soldiers since Fath's fath's father's day, maybe longer, and sometimes our women lay with them too, so blood got mixed and we were left alone. *Civitates*, they call us – citizen associates

– and now we were bringing a great big bell for one of their boats, cast on commission. Payment: a pretty bit.

We rested in milecastles, each eerily empty, to eat our slices of greasy mutton and drink the grain mash that made the growing snowdrifts tolerable. Only the Priest Popple refused to take the drink, saying it made a man turn.

Arriving in one such place we found a fellow wide of eye and hairy of chin.

'Tidings,' said Fath.

The man had in his hand a cudgel.

'No need for that,' said Fath. 'We're bringing a big bollocking bell for a boat that they say will sail to the emperor himself or thereabouts. What castle is this?'

Fath had all the milecastles memorised. The big forts too. Maia, Concavata, Aballava, Petrianis. These we had already passed close enough by to see that no smoke drifted upwards but not so close that we could tell whether they housed friendly faces.

Vercovicium was halfway across these open plains and the one that we had been told would welcome us with an eight-hundred-strong army who would replenish our supplies, for though this bell may have been moulded and hoisted by us Carvetii boys of the Carlisle locale, it was a returning empire merchant who had requested it and therefore warranted safe passage.

Strange that we had not yet seen any of these great soldiers who were said to be as tough as oak and the colour of this bronze bell. Strange indeed.

'Where are these men with their helmets of tin and broadswords you have told me many a tale about?' I had asked Fath.

'Might be that they've finally seen sense and left this land that is as cold as a tinker's tit,' he had replied.

'It's my castle,' the man growled in the accent of a fearsome Caledonian of the Borders. 'And you can ask a dozen dead men of Rome if you think otherwise.'

'We have empire passage,' said Fath.

'This is a Roman place no more. You'll give me all you have to eat and drink. And that girl.'

The Priest Popple stepped forward. 'With this cross of Jesu – '

The Caledonian struck out. He swung his cudgel and struck the Priest Popple on the temple and he fell like a scarecrow in a storm. Peg gasped. He twitched twice then did not move.

'Well, then,' said the Caledonian.

'This man has much meat in his bedroll,' said Fath. 'A jar too. Those and his clothes are yours in return for our passing.'

'What meat?'

'Good mutton. A side of ham too.'

'What jar?'

'Honey and oatmeal ale. The best there is.'

The fearsome Caledonian paused, then he stepped aside.

'I never much cared for that priest anyway,' said Fath as we walked on into the blizzard.

Whiteout.

We shared a tent that night. Me and Peg flanked Fath, and Foul Wendle lay long across our feet.

In the deepest part of night Peg said she needed to spill her waters and left, never to return.

The three of us went out looking for her in different directions, calling her name into the raging winds of a treacherous squall, our own noses barely visible. We saw nothing of my sister. The snow covered up her footprints and damn near buried the tent. Even the wall disappeared from view.

Only the bell guided us back. A fleeting shard of moonlight was enough to anchor us in this diabolical sea of rock and ice and we saw the bell glinting, a thing of beauty, set next to the creaking sanctuary of our cowhide shelter.

We never saw Peg again. She was lost to the land forever. Poor Peg, with roses in her cheeks and her life not yet lived.

No tears were shed that morning for that would have only made more ice for the world, but we took our victuals in solemn silence, warming our hands on the splinters of a burning wooden cross and hoping that the storm would return our Peg. It did not.

'We must honour my girl's death,' said Fath. 'And that of Colly and the Priest Popple too, though I grieve for neither. Soon we will be at Vercovicium, where it is said the stone floors are warmed by hidden fires and there is a room that makes a man sweat even when the sky is swirling sour outside.'

Fath and Wendle took the cart and we wordlessly continued.

Carvetii is our tribal name and it comes from *carvos*, meaning deer or stag. For stags we are. Wandering beasts, sleek and silent. Noble too. But on this day I knew what it was to be a pack-trail ass, dumb and bent double with the weight of my troubles, a blighted thing.

An arrow through the trunk of Foul Wendle was his undoing. From whence it came I know not, only that it flew twisting up over the jagged scarp somewhere north of the abandoned auxiliary fort of Vindolanda.

A miraculous shot, all told.

Fath folded the bellman's apprentice into his coat then laid him down in the shadows of the wall, away from further harm, and we both leaned in as death danced in his eyes like wet woodsmoke and a little black blood bubbled on his lips as he uttered his last words – something about that bloody bell that neither of us heard because the cruel wind stole even those.

Fath strapped his wrists to the cart handles with leather lanyard strips that blistered his skin. I pushed from the rear.

'How far to this fort, Fath?' I yelled to him, for the wind was up again.

'Not far now.'

'And you say the stone floors are warm to the touch there?'

Without looking back, Fath nodded into the storm.

'And there is enough food there to feed us for days?'

'Enough to feed an army.'

We were heaving the cart up a particularly steep and uneven section and I could see nothing but the cart and the back of Fath's head.

'And they will treat us well on account of this bloody great bell?'

'Son, when we've finished eating they'll have to roll us home.'

I smiled into the snow for I knew that better days were ahead.

Here Fath paused. As he took the strain of the cart I saw him look first to one side and then the other. Then again.

'No,' he cried out. '*No*. It cannot be. Oh, for the love of my dear dead wife and my dear dead daughter – it cannot be.'

I pushed through the snow to join him.

'What is wrong?'

'The wall,' he said.

'What about it?'

'Wedge the wheels of this cart and unstrap these handles.'

I found some stones the size of fists and pushed them beneath the handcart wheels and then loosened the leather strap on one of his hands. We leaned into the land.

Fath rubbed his wrist and then pointed through the streaming veils of thick white snow.

'Don't you see?'

I looked, then I looked again.

'The wall,' he said. 'It is to our right.'

'To the right?'

'We have crossed it,' said Fath, his voice raised again. 'We have crossed the wall and are going back on ourselves. Or perhaps we have crossed the wall twice. We are surely going in the wrong direction.'

'It can't be,' I said as a sob of desperation and fear welled up through my chest. 'It's true this bell is cursed indeed. It destroys everything in its path.'

And that was when the bell-laden cart start rolling backwards.

I turned to grab Fath but he was pulled away from me, the cart first dragging him by his one snared wrist and then flinging him up into the air as it flipped, and then bell, cart and man became one tumbling mess of wood and metal and flesh. Finally it came to a splintered rest deep in the drift of the wall.

I skidded down to where Father lay twisted and broken, his legs and arms at incomprehensible tangents.

I took the clapper from my back and beat the bell then. I struck it and hit it and smashed at it, and the sound of it rang out across the frozen northlands, but nothing happened and no one came, and I finally fell upon my father as the last warmth of him slipped away.

Ten Men

When Ray-Ray got out the second time he came to work on the farm.

He was brought in on the first warm breeze of the season with nothing but two carrier bags and a mean squint. He said he had heard we were hiring; he said he'd take any damn bloody thing going. As it happened, Uncle was short on labour for the coming season's grunt work so he gave him a pair of overalls and rigger boots and set him on there and then.

The days were extending. As spring slipped softly into summer, the sunlight was there for using and a hand could easily work twelve or fourteen hours, breaking off only for drink or bait, or to slink away behind a particular hedgerow with a woodbine and a dock leaf. Thinking time was what Uncle called it. He left a trowel back there.

Ray-Ray was a worker from the off. One of the best that he had ever seen, Uncle reckoned, and he was

as short on his compliments as he was of temper, so
you knew a good word that came from his mouth had
currency.

Uncle said that Ray-Ray might look like a runner bean
that had withered on a winter vine but that looks can be
deceptive, and it didn't take long to see that he had the
strength and stamina of ten men. Oftentimes you'll see
that it's the skinny ones who can keep on at it until the
moon is a pink pearl in the sky while the big beefcakes
who are throwing tyres like Frisbees all morning end up
bent double, spitting strings of breakfast bile on to their
toecaps by lunch. Big biceps count for squat out in the
fields, said Uncle. How long you can motor on down
the road for is all that matters. It's about the endurance.

———

Most of the other workers were itinerants, brought
on for short spells. There was a lot of foreign labour
then. Romanians, Czechs, some Albanians. Plenty of
Irish travellers too. Uncle didn't care for the whos, whys
and where-froms, though he always said that the Poles
were the best. The Poles could work like packhorses,
he reckoned, and they never meddled. Some of them
were building houses back home and they did the jobs
that many English lads simply wouldn't do, at twice the
speed and half the price, and never once complained
about their lot. Good boys, the Poles.

Mostly those that came in for picking and harvesting and baling were men with pasts that went unspoken. Men with secrets; men on the move.

Some, like Ray-Ray, had previously been detained at her majesty's leisure, while others were shedding old names that had been recorded for life in registers for reasons they did not care to reveal, reinventing themselves out in the fields. The few Englishmen who lasted to the season's limit were those who had already grown up with dirt streaking the lines of their hands, and who didn't have much of a compulsion to try anything else, for their lives were locked into older agricultural ways, their roots running deep through generations. They were in the soil and the soil was in them, though they were in the minority now and, as the song said, the times they were a-changing.

———————

Ray-Ray had the good sense to keep to himself. Daytimes he worked the fields and nights he spent in the static van hunched over a little black-and-white portable that you had to tune with a dial. He didn't drink away his brown envelope like the rest of the hands, who supped their week's earnings in town each Saturday night, then went at it with the local toughs on the cobbles before spending the next seven days sweating and cursing through dry mouths of bitter regret in the fields, only to do it all over again come the weekend. No, Ray-Ray kept his head down.

Spring through summer was spent ploughing furrows and baling hay, topping haulm or rinsing turnips. Whatever Uncle required. Down south our Kentish farming counterparts worked the hops too, but not up here in the northlands, where the soil is bad for all that, and they say the sun doesn't burn so hot either.

The men worked. The men drank. They bickered and they ate well, and for the most part they sorted out their differences the old way, bone on bone, with blackened eyes sported like medals.

Then later, as autumn beckoned, when the last grass had been stored and the cows brought in, and a wood-pile the size of a bungalow had been built with logs split from trunks that Uncle had us drag up mob-handed from the oxbow bend on the floodplain, the foreign men scattered to the four corners of the compass for the winter.

Occasionally in October picking time a few of the English workers might stay on to spend their days up rusty ladders in the old orchard snatching apples from the breeze before the worms moved in and the first frost hit, but that harvest was a shortening window and by then most had already moved on, to rented flats and seaside caravan parks, to estates and hostels and tower blocks. To malnourished children and mean-eyed women awaiting a summer's wages already supped and spent.

Not Ray-Ray, though. Ray-Ray stayed. Uncle said he could stop in the static so long as he didn't mind the cracked glass and the perishing cold, or expect work when the rutted furrows were under a rink of ice and the barn beasts were lowing, and there was little for a man to do after the milking except dream of the endless golden days of summer to come.

He fixed the place up good. He scrubbed off the mildew with a bucket of bleach and patched up that cracked window with cardboard and tape. There was a wood-burner in there that provided heat and space for one-pot cooking, and Uncle gave him cords of logs and kindling too.

Now and again Ray-Ray would let me into the van and once he gave me a tin of dimps to break down and rake out on a sheet of newspaper for re-rolling, the bitter twists of half-burned tobacco shredded and mixed and then shredded again, the recycled smoke turning my young tongue a mustard yellow.

I was eleven then and had already been nailing the tabs two years.

He said little but when I asked him why he was called Ray-Ray he told me he was named Raymond Raymond Robinson, after both his father, Raymond Robinson Jr, and his grandfather, also Raymond Robinson. That made him Ray-Ray Jr Jr and I think his mother must have liked the name because it stuck like a burr, but when I said as much he just shrugged and replied that it wasn't the worst he'd had done to him.

He was also the first man I'd seen who had tattoos up his forearms – just his forearms, though – so that when he stripped shirtless in the sticky summer months he looked odd with his white biceps and hairless chest ink-free, his torso gradually browning as the shadows of the seasons stretched long, but his lower arms busy with swallows and skulls and names and dates on them, and strange sigils and insignias that I inherently understood represented nothing good.

One time I knocked on for him but Ray-Ray didn't answer, so I banged harder and eventually the door swung open and he leaned there in the doorway, blocking it and squinting as if the sun was in his face even though it was a damp November morning with a fine mizzle falling, and when he said what is it that you're wanting and I said nothing Ray-Ray, I saw a tinder spark of anger flash behind his eyes.

Go play round your own doors, then.

When he went back inside I thought I heard the voice of someone else in there but I couldn't be sure because by then he had pinned old sheets to the insides of his windows, and something in his voice told me not to meddle.

———————

A week or so after that it started snowing and it didn't let up for two whole days and nights.

First the flakes fell straight down, fat and gentle, and then they blew in sideways, whipping across the fields to rattle the corrugated sheets of the barns and sheds and pelt the farmhouse windows, and it came in so dark you could barely see the dim light from the battery lamp that hung in Ray-Ray's van across the yard.

In the morning I went to see him but there was no answer. I tried the door and when it opened of its own accord I was met by a slightly sour smell hanging in there. Clothes were scattered on the floor and dirty sauce-stained plates were stacked tilted in the tiny sink; Ray-Ray's water came from an outside tap and plastic bottles of different sizes stood around the van.

I stepped inside.

I knew that I shouldn't be in his private space; the thump of my heart in my eardrums told me so. I knew too that I was encroaching, and that could bring about trouble. He had once told me that in prison a man never walks into another's cell without being invited because it is such rituals and considerations that maintain a semblance of order under cramped conditions. Every man needs his cave and to cross his threshold unasked brings trouble, Ray-Ray said, yet here I was wandering into his home.

A shaft of dull light crept in through a narrow gap where one of the sheets had come free and dust danced there. But still I didn't leave.

The wardrobe door was ajar. I opened it with the tip of one finger.

In it there hung a pair of coveralls, a padded plaid work shirt and a dress.

189

I leaned into the darkness and touched the dress, then pressed my face to it, smelling the scent of Ray-Ray's secret girlfriend in a cocktail of citrus-sharp perfume, smoke and the dried remnants of sticky drinks spilled in the after-hours hinterlands of bars and clubs, places I did not understand but knew existed out there beyond the barbed-wire fences and five-bar gates that were the limit of my life then.

The feminine odours were an intrusion amongst the rank stench of cow scat and rotting mulch piles that sat in the farm's barns or trickled down its silage drains, this world of men, and in that moment deep within me was evoked a distant memory of a mother I had barely known, and whose face I could not recall. In that scent she came back to me, briefly reanimated.

As I tramped back to the house I felt exhilarated and glad of the fresh falling snow that would cover the guilty footprints of a bored and curious boy stuck out there in the remote pastures of the north country, searching for meaning on the blank canvas of winter.

Christmas came and Uncle slaughtered a suckling pig and roasted a few geese that he had been fattening with a grain mix that he liked to dash with cheap rum.

That night we were joined in the kitchen by a number of neighbours, many of whom had trudged across the fields to feast, and on Boxing Day we rose early to load up the truck with sacks of logs, plastic jugs of a home-brewed cider that Unc called Lightmeup and which he spiced himself with cloves and raisins soaked in spirits, and leftover cold cuts wrapped up in greaseproof paper, and we took them to the furthest-flung families of the valley, where fathers were out of work, injured, signed off, incarcerated or absent.

Ray-Ray rode with us, smoking out the window, and when we stopped he threw down supplies for me to take to the doors of these places of poverty and want, where families existed in isolation, who rarely saw a city. At each we were offered nips of whiskey or pouches of tobacco or jars of jam. Everyone knew Uncle; his name was good.

When he and Ray-Ray declined a drink the women pressed slices of fruit cake wrapped in thick marzipan or twists of paper containing nuts and raisins into my hands instead. At one house I was gifted a brand-new hand-knitted scarf.

On the morning of New Year's Eve, I was up early to muck out the pigs and do all my usual chores when a man appeared in the yard. He nodded at me.

'Looking for a lad by the name of Ray-Ray.' When I didn't reply he said: 'Do you know him?'

Even then I understood that to be a man of the world was to say little and be discreet at all times. Sometimes a grunt or a look was enough. Always best to let others do the talking, Unc said.

I pointed to his van.

The man turned.

'There, is he?'

I shrugged.

'A friend, are you?' I said.

'We were inside as kids,' he said. 'Then later I celled with him in Durham. Is he here, then?'

I shrugged again.

'Bloody hillbillies,' he muttered, and then walked to the van.

———

The snow came down thicker that evening and I watched from my window as it silently settled on the hardened crust of ice. It sat on the power lines and blanketed the muddy morass of the yard.

Uncle let me stay up until after midnight, the two of us staring into the banked fire, flinching as the logs hissed and popped, until finally he stood and said well, that's another one gone, and then climbed the creaking stairs to a bedroom I never saw.

I could not sleep. In the deepest part of night, when all was still and white, I heard a skein of migrating geese fly overhead and then just moments later a cough followed by footsteps. I parted the curtain and saw two women tottering through the snow and into the yard.

They were drunk as owls and unsteady on the ice. They held their coats shut and clung to each other.

Flakes of snow had settled into their styled hair. Their heels imprinted tiny dots in the fresh white carpet.

The two women went into Ray-Ray's static caravan and shut the door behind them. Minutes passed as I watched the faint light flickering through the snow-thick night and it was like that of a lighthouse seen by a solitary lovesick sailor from far out at sea. I wondered if it was true that the architecture of each flake was unique.

The night was too alive and my mind too curious for sleep so I climbed out from under my blankets and pulled on my clothes. Downstairs, the fire was still glowing in the grate and the front room was so warm that I hesitated there for a moment. Then I opened the door and went into the yard.

The snow sat shin-deep and was still coming down, the flakes spinning silently, the light a strange shade of darkened purple, like a two-day bruise.

The snow came in over my boots. I was not wearing any socks.

As I crossed the yard to the van I heard the jostle and clatter of the cows in their shed, and the occasional snort.

Ray-Ray's van sat low in the snow, as if the ground were consuming it slowly. I went to the window, taking quiet high steps through the drifts that had curled up to the side of it.

Gentle music came from within. Treading slowly and carefully, I looked through the tiny gap between the hung sheets and saw that the inside of the van was lit by candles in glass bottles, the wicks flickering as oily white wax dripped down their necks.

One of the women had her back to me and was obscuring my view. I held my breath so as not to steam the glass as she laughed and tipped her head back, and then stood, swaying slightly on muscular hairy legs.

I saw then sitting opposite her was Ray-Ray in the same dress that had been hanging in his wardrobe. A wig was on the table before him, splayed like the pelt of a skinned animal, his bare arms carrying the strength of ten men, those familiar tattoos telling the narrative of his life.

He too was laughing as he brought his lighter up to the stub of his cigarette, and around me the silent snow fell thicker still.

The Astronaut

After he had looked back at the earth from the surface of the moon, his entire perspective changed. Suddenly the little things in life – golf, haircuts, birthday parties – seemed to be robbed of all meaning.

Friends and family back home thought that space travel might have given him a greater appreciation for the minutiae of existence. Even the scientists, humbled by the magnitude of the successful mission, were prone to such sentimentality, but in fact the astronaut found he experienced quite the opposite. Now when he looked at his fellow humans he felt only a sense of deflation and disdain.

After the initial swell of publicity receded, he went into freefall. His world shrank. He drank. He went from being an astronaut to a former astronaut and he felt far more alone than he had while perilously floating 238,000 miles above all that he knew.

Everyone asked him the same thing: 'What was it like,' they wondered, 'to walk on the moon?' Everywhere he went. In restaurants, at petrol pumps, even at urinals. Unable to succinctly encapsulate this awesome spectacle against the banal backdrop of modern earthly life, especially while urinating, he took to hurrying away, mumbling, the front of his trousers spotted with unwanted droplets.

To millions he was a hero whose footprint was one of the first to grace the moon's surface, but most mornings he couldn't get out of bed. Everything was exhausting.

His wife left him for a granola salesman with a pug and a trike. He saw his children twice a month on Sundays.

Such trouble adjusting to normality is common among astronauts, for in their hearts there is a vortex as bottomless as a black hole and in their eyes the dying embers of fading stars.

Bomber

That final night Bomber had an argument with Karen in the pub. It was very vocal and involved much waving of limbs and wagging of digits, mainly on her part. Everyone heard it, and those who didn't hear it saw it from the street as they skidded by on the frosted flagstones of the city's old pavement, such was the ferocity of Karen's gesticulations, accusations and all-round character assassination.

She was sick of his shit. Sick of his drinking and staying out all night; sick of the greasy bike parts in the front room and the unkept promise of taking her away somewhere nice like Cornwall or Greece.

After a minute or two of this, Bomber gave up on defending himself and stopped speaking entirely, affecting a studied air of nonchalance. Sitting on his usual stool at the bar and looking around the room with deliberate indifference, overly impervious to her litany

of complaints, he casually raised his pint of heavy and
drained it in two gulps.

To anyone who knew him it was just Bomber being
Bomber. Unfazed. Cool as.

Only when he smirked and Karen tried to claw his
face, and she had to be pulled back by Andy, Mad Neil
and Rasputin, did he seem rattled.

After she had been bustled away into the snug and
brought a double Midori to help calm her down,
Bomber threaded his bare arms back into his leather
jacket, jerked it into place and, though he was only four
pints into what had otherwise been shaping up to be a
promising Friday night, left.

He went straight home and painted himself black.

The decision wasn't racially motivated; skin colour
was never a consideration, and Bomber would have
fervently argued his defence if anyone had thought
otherwise. Midnight Black Gloss was simply the only
tin of paint he had to hand, and to cover himself
in it seemed like the perfect protest against Karen's
public humiliation of him in front of his friends and
no short number of strangers. It was a bold declaration, a very visual statement of his daring and sheer
fuck-offness, for which he believed himself to be
widely admired.

Bomber slid a live Motörhead bootleg into the stereo
and then went upstairs, took his clothes off, climbed
into the bath and with a brush began to carefully baste
himself in the thick paint, stopping now and again to

take hearty glugs from a ten-glass bottle of whiskey that was left over from last Christmas.

He worked from the ankles up, covering the curves of his calves and his thick white thighs, his cock and balls. He liked the way the hairs on his body looked beneath the obsidian sheen of the paint. Bomber kept going and though the whiskey was cheap, it went down. A mixer would have been nice, he thought, but he was too far into his self-decoration to break the creative flow. Instead he added a little cold water to the bottle from the bath tap.

His arms and hands were harder to do as he had to keep switching the brush from left hand to right, and he only managed to paint his shoulders and part of his lower back so that a large section of it was untouched save for a few messy smears, but by that time he was very drunk, the fumes were making him feel slightly strange and his technique was becoming sloppy.

His chest felt tight.

A cigarette, he reasoned. A cigarette would mask the stench and clear the pipes.

Bomber painted his entire face quickly. From neck to chin, chin to retreating hairline. He even did his eyelids and ears, then threw the brush into the sink and on unsteady legs climbed out of the bath.

He looked in the mirror and was thrilled by his reflection. Proud of his inventiveness, his handiwork. He was a new man. A better man. He looked like a bloody Greek god or something.

He shouted for Karen, but then remembered that Karen wasn't home yet, so he padded downstairs on the only parts of him except his arse cheeks that were still entirely white. It was cold so he turned the gas fire on, went to the kitchen and lit a cigarette from the hob, and then walked back into the front room.

Motörhead were still chugging away at great volume on the stereo. Between songs the crowd roared their approval.

'Do you crazy motherfuckers want some more?' Lemmy bellowed.

Yes, the crowd collectively responded. We are indeed crazy and we would very much like some more.

The bars of the electric fire created a soft, cosy light in the still winter darkness that only made Bomber's new black coating appear more brilliant. He examined his arms and legs as if they belonged to someone else, and they glowed with a golden hue. He was a beautiful sculpture, a memorial to original thinking, and he would have a drink to celebrate. But the bottle was upstairs and now he was very dizzy. The cigarette didn't seem to have helped with his breathing either – inhaling the smoke had only made him more aware of the narrowness of his gullet, the smallness of his lungs – and his whole body felt odd, as if a hundred tourniquets were being tied around him at once, and everything was tightening and hardening.

Pounding wildly, Bomber's heart felt cornered in the cage of his chest like a trapped rat. He was feeling very dizzy indeed.

His legs crumpled then, but he managed to sit himself down in the chair in front of the fire. The music was too loud, and Lemmy's engine-like bass guitar, a dirty gurgle that had consistently thrilled him for nearly thirty years, now sounded toxic, like an exhaust pipe was filling the room with sound. His body prickled all over, as if dirty needles were being jabbed into the drying crust of the Midnight Black Gloss.

Bomber wanted to turn the music off but found that he could not move. His body refused to follow the command of his mind and the music only added to the anxiety that was now engulfing him.

Lost within his own body, his breath was becoming thinner and thinner. He back-belched whiskey, and a little bit of sour vomit flooded his mouth. It took every effort to swallow it. The fire was hot. Too hot.

The music was loud. Too loud.

Bomber's breath shrank to a hopeless rasp. He was in a prison of dry paint that had blocked all of his pores. He was suffocating in himself, his head throbbing with a noxious chemical fervour.

Then the heat from the fire was burning the paint on his shins. Blister bubbles were speckling the layer of black lacquer and his bones felt like they were being gnawed, but still he could not move. He was mummifying.

His breath became first a silent shriek and then a sigh in the raw corridor of his throat. He exhaled like a busted squeezebox.

'Thank you, goodnight,' said Lemmy, just seconds before Karen slipped her key into the lock, walked into the house and found Bomber sitting stiff and upright in the chair, his hands on the armrests, white eyes pulled wide open and staring at the mantelpiece, on which there sat a box of matches, three spent candles, a wrench, an engine gasket, several wing nuts, some loose change and a faded postcard of the Parthenon.

Snorri & Frosti

Snorri and Frosti are brothers.

They live in a wooden cabin on a remote hillside above a village in a northern European country. They are in their seventies. Snorri is the elder of the pair by two years. The cabin has one bedroom, a kitchen and one main room with a wood-burning stove in it. They have lived there all of their lives. Snow covers the surrounding slopes for more than half the year. Snorri and Frosti chop wood for people and tend to the land for a living. Once a week they walk into town to buy supplies.

It is winter. It is cold. Frosti has a headache.

I. BREAKFAST

Are you awake?

. . .

Snorri.

. . .

Snorri.

Yes.

Are you awake?

No.

There's been a big fall in the night, Snorri. Look how light the room is. Hear how the world is muffled.

I'm sleeping.

Brother, I can't sleep. I have been awake for a long time, just lying here, not moving, except for my toes. I think the snow will be up to the porch today.

. . .

I said I think the snow will be up to the porch.

Frosti.

Yes.

Go and see the snow if you like. But I am sleeping.

That's OK. The snow can wait.

Then light the fire.

I think I'd like to just lie here a little longer and enjoy the silence.

What silence?

The silence of the valley.

I don't hear silence. All I hear is you.

Can you even hear silence? That's my question. I am not so sure that silence can even make a sound.

Now you're being pedantic. Let me sleep. It is too early for this type of discussion.

Sometimes the silence is deafening, Snorri. I find that odd. That silence can ring in your ears.

That is a contradiction.

You have never stood in the wood and listened to the roar of silence?

Yes. Yes, I have.

Then you know what I mean, Snorri.

Yes. I do.

Today the silence is deafening. I can hear it. And the early-morning fall is so fresh and the sun so low over the ridge that the snow is as pink as a side of salmon.

. . .

Snorri.

What now.

I think I'm going to go and light the fire after all.

So light the fire.

Are you going back to sleep?

I'm awake now. But I may have another ten minutes.

You used to get up two hours before daylight.

I used to do a lot of things. We're old men now.

Speak for yourself.

I don't speak for anyone else.

You know, sometimes I wake up and for a few moments I think I am a teenager again. Sometimes I feel like I am a young man and all the people who have died are still here, and I have my whole life ahead of me. Then I remember.

Sleep plays tricks.

Yes, it does. Sometimes sleep is like time travel. I'm going to light the fire now.

Did you hear the geese in the night, Frosti?

No. I missed them. I always miss them.

One day.
One day.

———

It is your turn to make the coffee.

I believe I made the coffee yesterday, Snorri.

No. I think you are wrong there, little brother.

In this instance I think it is *you* that is wrong. I specifically remember because I spilled a little hot water on my hand.

I don't remember that.

It blistered.

Let me see.

Here – take a look.

That's not a blister, Frosti.

Yes, it is.

No, that is a callus.

I scalded my hand.

Maybe you did. But that is a callus. Look: I have one too, in the exact same place, but on my other hand. We both know where they came from.

Did you spill hot water on yourself too, Snorri?

Funny. That's funny. No, mine is from the axe, Frosti. And so is yours. If it were a blister it would be as white as the snow and full of liquid. That mark is dry and hard. It is a callus. It is your turn to make the coffee.

But I made it yesterday.

Must we go through this every morning.

If it is to prove that I am right, then yes, I suppose so.

If I make the coffee then you have to make it tomorrow and then the day after that.

Why?

It is like a debt, says Snorri.

A debt?

Yes. Because I will then have done it two days running and the cost of that to you is that you then have to make the coffee for two days. I should be charging interest.

Interest.

Yes.

How?

I don't know. Maybe you should have to light the fire that day too. It would be a penalty for avoiding your duty.

But I made it yesterday.

How do I know you are not just saying this to get one over on me?

Dear brother. How could you say such a thing.

I know what you are like, Frosti. You do these things for your own amusement. You like to think you are fooling me, but we know you are not.

We can't be certain.

Well, says Snorri.

Well, says Frosti.

I'm cold. I need coffee. Will you make it, Frosti?

OK. Just this once I will make it. But if I scald myself again it will be your fault.

Why would you?

I don't know. Sometimes these things just happen.

Well, take care pouring the water into the coffee pot and you will be alright.

OK. I'm going to make the coffee now, Snorri. How would you like it?

How would I like it?

Yes.

You know how I like it.

I do? says Frosti.

I have been drinking it the same way for sixty years. As have you. Now I know you are trying to make a fool out of me again.

I thought this time you might like a drop of milk in it.

After sixty years of taking it black you suddenly ask me if I would like it with milk?

Yes.

But we do not have milk.

Maybe we do.

But we don't, says Snorri.

No. Perhaps not.

Have you acquired a cow in the night?

No, but –

Then we do not have milk. Look, the longer you talk, Frosti, the colder we get. The fire is just at the right temperature for coffee. See how the logs are glowing white and the embers are dancing up the flue?

Is that right?

Yes. I'm usually right. You should know that by now.

One day you will be wrong.

We'll see, Frosti. We shall see.

I'll make the coffee now, Snorri, but tomorrow you will make it.

Tomorrow is another day.

You will get no argument from me about that. Once again you are right.

Thank you. Careful you don't scald yourself.

———

See how the snow falls, Snorri.

I see.

Oh boy. It's really coming down.

Never goes up.

That thing about no two flakes being the same, says Frosti. Do you think that's actually true?

We have no way of knowing.

You'd have to compare every single snowflake that is falling to one another.

Yes.

That would be madness, says Frosti.

Yes.

And not just every single snowflake that is falling but every snowflake that ever fell, and ever will fall.

Yes.

They would melt before you could do that.

Yes, says Snorri.

All my life I've been watching snow and I never tire of it.

I'll tell you something, little brother. Don't they say that over in Greenland the Eskimos have dozens of words for snow?

I believe they say that, yes.

Well, that's not true, says Snorri. They have many words for different types of snow, or the conditions in which the snow is created, or the variations of snow, just as we do. But only really a handful of words for snow in its simple, basic form.

I bet someone who doesn't live in the snow made that up, Snorri. Southerners.

Probably. Everyone knows it's not the Eskimos anyway but the Sámi that have many words for snow. Hundreds of them.

These people that say these things must be idiots, says Frosti.

Yes. Even the little child just starting school knows this. But out there in the world these ideas get passed around and suddenly they become fact even if they are not true.

They should do their homework.

The children?

No, the idiots who say these things about snow.

You're right, Frosti.

It's really heavy today. It has been falling for two weeks straight now.

We'd worry if it wasn't.

That's true.

Big flakes. See how the fall sits on the bough of the tree.

Like frozen smoke from an underground chimney, Snorri.

And see how the tree fattens and strains under the weight.

Like Harold the Baker.

I see what you mean.

The trouble with Harold is he eats too much of his own produce.

Yes.

And now he's a bloated triangle, like that pine. His grey hair makes him even more so.

I like Harold.

I like Harold too, Snorri, but he should cut down on his sweet buns. I heard they are bad for the heart.

Maybe.

It's really coming down now.

Doesn't go up.

Will we still go chopping today?

Of course, Frosti. Why wouldn't we? It's not stopped us yet.

Sometimes I just like to watch it fall.

I know you do, Frosti.

I often think this must be how some people feel about their televisions. Like they could sit and watch them all day.

Yes.

But I don't think television programmes are like snowflakes.

Well, yes.

Because they show the same shows over and over again. You don't get that with snowflakes.

No, Frosti. You don't.

Also, there is only one word for television.

True. You should finish your oatmeal and get ready.

Let me just watch a little longer, Snorri. I've not seen this programme before.

———

Snorri, I was thinking.

You're always thinking, Frosti. Too much thinking can be a distraction. You know, sometimes it is fine to just *be*.

Thinking gets me through the day. When I'm chopping wood, I mean. That's when I do all my best thinking. That and on the toilet. But only in the summer. Wintertime you can't hang about on the thunderbox.

So.

So I was thinking about how I think I'd like to build a sweat lodge. When the spring thaw comes, I mean.

You say this every year, Frosti. Always when the snow is thickest on the ground.

I do?

Yes. You know you do.

Because I'm fairly certain that the thought just came to me this morning.

Trust me. You've had this idea before.

I really don't recall.

I do.

212

Oh.

Yes.

Still, though. It's a good idea, isn't it? I'd like to build it the old way.

Which way do you mean? says Snorri.

Well, first we'd need to dig a pit –

We?

Yes, we. You and me.

So suddenly I'm building the sweat lodge too, Frosti?

It's for both of us. We could both use it.

Go on.

So we dig the pit. Not too wide, not too deep. Just deep enough to sit in. Then we make a roof for the pit, but with a hatch or doorway to climb in and out. We could cover the roof with soil too, to make it more efficient. To disguise it.

Why would we need to disguise it?

I don't know. That's just how I picture it in my mind.

OK.

Somehow I see it as an underground sweat lodge.

Right.

Then what you do is you build a nice big fire nearby and then when it has settled down you put some stones in the ashes.

I know how a sweat lodge works, Frosti.

River stones are best. Nice smooth round ones. When they are hot – I mean really hot, Snorri – you then move them down on to the floor of the lodge, where we'll have cut out a sort of hole within a hole. A little fireplace.

How will we move them?

A bucket should do it. Then you ladle some cold water on the heap of hot stones to create the steam. Then you sit back and sweat it out.

I have to admit, it does sound nice.

Refreshing.

Yes, refreshing, Frosti.

Like being cleaned from the inside out.

Yes.

It would be dark in the sweat lodge but that wouldn't be a problem because we would have candles in there. And anyway, what does a bit of darkness matter when you feel so good.

And then when you've sweated as much as you can stand –

Well, that's the best bit, Snorri. When you've sweated as much as you can stand you jump in the lake.

But the lake is five kilometres away.

So we build the sweat lodge close to the lake. Or beside the stream. It would still give you a nice jolt. It's not a problem, dear brother.

And you're going to do all this, Frosti?

Sure. As soon as the snow melts.

Is this before or after the toboggan run?

Which toboggan run?

The one you were threatening to make just two months ago.

Oh, that.

Or the ice cave you were going to carve and fill with your own line-caught spring salmon that you never catch. Or the boat you were going to build to sail to the island on the lake.

Well.

Where you would sleep in the tent you were going to hand-stitch.

OK.

Or the bees you were going to keep for honey.

Bees aren't so easy to keep.

You may need to start soon, Frosti. You are seventy-five years old.

I do not see age as a barrier. In old age we are like a batch of letters that someone has sent. We are no longer in the past, we have arrived. I read that somewhere. I live in the present moment.

Well, so do I, but laziness could be a hindrance.

You think I am lazy?

No, actually I don't. The way you chop wood is admirable. And you help run a fine house. You have worked the land all your life, of that there is little doubt. But you are a dreamer, Frosti. Every year you have these winter dreams.

Winter dreams?

Yes. These ambitious visions. These grand plans that never reach fruition. Winter dreams.

You say that like it is a bad thing, Snorri. Tomorrow I will rise and make coffee and chop wood, but today I shall dream. It is what I am good at.

You take after Father. And you do it very well. What you are not so good at is making sweat lodges, boats, ice caves, tents, toboggan runs and beehives.

One day, Snorri. One day.

After the spring thaw?

Sure, why not. Then we'll see who's laughing.

I'm not laughing.

Yes, but I will be laughing. I will be laughing and sweating and telling you to fetch another bucket of ice-cold water from the mountain stream.

Frosti. If you make this sweat lodge that you have been talking about for as long as I can remember now, I will gladly fetch you the bucket of water. I will bring you a thousand buckets of water. I will put them in my brand-new toboggan and the bees will give me a push.

You're mocking me now, Snorri. But one day.

After the spring thaw?

After the spring thaw.

I shall look forward to it.

———

Do you know what I like most about coffee?

If I said, I would only be guessing, Frosti.

So guess.

I don't know.

Come on, Snorri. A conversation needs two people.

I don't know. The taste?

Wrong. Guess again.

I don't know. The way it warms you up when it's fifteen below, as it surely is this morning?

Nope, though I do like that. Again.

Come on, Frosti, I don't have time for this. There is work to be done. You're acting like a child.

Just one more guess.

No. I need to get ready. See how the sun is climbing.

It's my movements, Snorri. I like the way it helps my morning movements.

Do I need to know this when I have been living with you all these years?

Regularity leads to good health, Snorri. That's all.

Brother, the walls of this cabin are thin. I know enough about you as it is. Please.

There's something about coffee. The way it flushes you out like that.

Frosti. That's enough.

I'm just saying.

I think I'd rather you didn't. Civilised beings don't need to discuss these things at the breakfast table.

You can set your watch by it.

You don't have a watch, Frosti.

Ah, well, you see. That's because I don't need one. I have coffee. My body is my clock.

Well, then your body should tell you that soon we will be late. I am going to work now.

Me too, Snorri.

But you're not ready. You don't even have your boots on.

I'm right behind you.

If I set off now you won't catch me up.

Yes, I will.

No, you won't.

Yes, I will. I just need to do my ablutions.

Ablutions. You will have to run to catch me and the drifts lie deep this morning, brother. You're not getting any younger, Frosti.

Well, wait for me, then.

But then I will be late. The doctor will not be pleased.

You are working the doctor's land today?

Yes.

So go, then.

You don't want me to wait?

Yes, I would like you to wait.

But then I will be late, Frosti.

I can't find my boots. Have you seen my boots?

They should be drying by the burner, where they always are.

They are not there.

Then I do not know. Have you got your morning snack?

Not yet.

Brother, you have been daydreaming again.

I have a headache this morning.

Any excuse.

No really, Snorri. My head really does ache this morning. Even just to look at the snow hurts my eyes.

Perhaps you are coming down with something.

Perhaps.

Do you hurt anywhere else?

No. Just my head.

It will pass.

I hope so.

I will wait for you, Frosti. We can walk together.

Thank you, Snorri.

That's OK.

———

The snow is bright this morning.

The snow is bright most mornings, Frosti. Today it is no brighter than usual.

Then it's this headache. The snow doesn't even look white today.

What colour does it look?

I don't know. It just hurts to look at it.

Maybe you have snow blindness.

After all these years, I doubt it. It's as if it is something more than white today. A sort of painful purity.

Painful purity? Well now, what grand talk. Suddenly you're a poet.

I feel a little tired today too.

You woke early.

I couldn't sleep.

You were dreaming again?

Yes. I dream, then I wake up and the thought of the dream, and the light that the snow casts in the room, prevents me from getting back to sleep. I think perhaps we need new curtains, Snorri.

I think perhaps you need a new head. Our curtains are fine.

I don't feel like chopping too much today.

Brother, you must be unwell. This is not like you.

I feel like maybe chopping a few logs, but not too many. I won't be setting any world records.

You're doing OK, Frosti. We both are. We might be old men but our bodies are holding out. Our name is still good.

Seventy years I've swung the axe, over sixty of those professionally.

Yes.

And today I am thinking that perhaps it is becoming a little repetitive.

It is your headache, Frosti. It's making you say these things.

Maybe. You don't find the chopping repetitive?

No.

Never?

Never, says Snorri. Why would I?

I don't know.

Sometimes I just wonder.

About what?

Things.

Things?

You know, just –

Look, Frosti, this is where I head off.

OK, Snorri.

Perhaps we can talk about this later.

Perhaps.

I'll see you.

Yes.

At the house.

Yes.

For lunch.

And coffee.

And coffee.

II. LUNCH

There he is. My little brother Frosti with the big axe. So how much wood did you chop this morning?

This morning I chopped some thirty metres of trunk. And I split a good many logs for kindling. They'll season nicely.

The widow must be pleased.

Her fire need never go out for many months. At ten o'clock she brought me cake. And what about you, Snorri? What did you do?

This morning I dug out that spruce stump.

The one on the doctor's land?

One and the same. I could have done with your help with it. It was a two-man job.

I bet the pay is not that of two men.

You're right there, Frosti. The doctor is a good man, but he is not generous with his payments. He even asked me to chop the stump for his woodpile. I will do that later.

Well.

Well.

But why have you to dig out the stump now, Snorri, when the ground is frozen hard?

It seems the doctor intends to plant a new vegetable patch on the land and needs to turn the soil in time for spring. I had to build a fire over the stump to defrost the soil. That took up half the morning. But I cooked some chestnuts in there to pass the time. They were as sweet as Belgian chocolate.

The doctor's vegetable patch will fail. I like him, but his vegetables will fail. If a spruce cannot grow there, what hope do turnips have?

I agree, Frosti. But what can you do. People need to make their own mistakes.

That land has been untillable for a long time.

Yes.

And every spring the thaw waters flood the low patches.

Yes.

The doctor should know this, Snorri.

The doctor spends his days behind a desk. The doctor is very good at his job.

Yes. And we are good at ours.

No one can chop wood like us, eh, Frosti?

Everyone knows it.

Between us we must have chopped a dozen forests.

More, Snorri. More. Before I could read I could chop.

I remember. Father gave you your first axe at the age of five. A short-handle with a blade as thin as a man could forge by hand and heat, it was. I already had my own, of course. The way you wielded it –

Impressive?

For a little one, yes. You got a good heft on it, even then. People would joke about it. They would say see how little Frosti swings his blade. They'd come from the village to see you make splinters. They would say he's going to grow up to be big and strong, that one.

And I did.

And you did. Mother had to stop you from taking your axe to school in your lunch bag.

That is true. I always feel good with an axe in my hand.

Sometimes I feel the same. The world is full of uncertainty, change and confusion but there is truth in an axe blade.

Yes, Snorri. The axe never lies.

It simply chops.

So long as it is regularly sharpened and oiled very occasionally, a good axe should last a lifetime.

And there will always be trees that need chopping, logs that need splitting. So long as people need fire and wood for their cabins and tables and chairs, there will always be work for men like us.

Men like us. I hope so, Snorri.

But we are old now.

Yes. But my aim is still true. So long as it is I will keep swinging my axe. I'd rather die than stop.

Death may have to stop you, Frosti. It stops everyone in the end.

Yes.

Death and the axe blade are the only certain truths in
this strange life.

And taxes. Don't forget taxes, Snorri.

Yes. Taxes too.

It's a shame we can't pay our taxes in woodchips.

Yes. If woodchips were coins we'd be rich men.

And that's the truth of it.

———

There is stew in the pot, Frosti.

What kind?

Ham hock and vegetable.

My favourite.

I put a dash of paprika in. And how is your head now,
brother?

It still hurts.

You need food.

Yes.

Have you had enough water?

I don't know.

Drink some water and I will make the coffee.

OK.

I'll fetch you a slice of rye bread.

Thank you.

Here you are.

Thanks. I fell this morning, Snorri.

You fell.

Yes. On the ice.

Did you hurt yourself?

My hip will be bruised by sundown.

I expect I would have heard by now if anything had broken.

Yes. I imagine you would, Snorri.

How is your stew?

It needs more salt.

———

Tell me about the Hotel Dulac.

Again?

Yes.

Sometimes I wonder about you, Frosti.

I like to hear the story while we eat.

You know the story inside out and back to front.

You eat oatmeal every day.

So?

So I like to hear it. Is there anything so wrong with that? It's a good story.

OK.

But from the beginning.

OK, Frosti. The Hotel Consort is in the capital city –

I said from the beginning. Please tell me about the journey.

The journey.

Yes.

Starting where?

At the beginning.

But where? Where is the beginning? Do you want me to go back to the point of my birth?

There is no need for sarcasm, Snorri. From when you left here is fine.

Fine. So I walked into town.

What was the weather like?

Cold as always, but clear. There had been a big fall in the night, but the skies were blue with patches of only the very lightest clouds. The sun was large and white. It cast the snow pink.

Good.

I slipped once or twice but I did not fall. I had my backsack with me.

With a change of clothes in.

Yes. With a change of clothes in.

And your toothbrush, of course, Snorri.

When I got into the village I met the postman.

Stefan.

Yes. Stefan the postman. A good man. A heavy drinker but a good man.

With a beer belly.

Yes. Stefan with the beer belly, though not as big a belly as Harold the Baker. Anyway, after he had run some errands he kindly drove me into town.

Did you get a flat tyre on the way?

You know we did, Frosti. Fortunately Stefan had a spare in the boot –

And one round his waist.

And after only a ten-minute break he changed it and we were on our way again.

It took one and one half hours to drive into town.

It took longer than that, Frosti.

Last time you told me it took one and one half hours to drive into town, Snorri.

OK. So it took one and one half hours to drive into town, plus ten minutes to change the tyre.

Tell me what you did when you got there.

I bought Stefan a cup of coffee.

Where?

In a cafe.

Which one?

The Hot Food Cafe.

Good. Did you eat?

Stefan ordered eggs.

And you?

I just had coffee. Afterwards Stefan smoked a cigarette.

But you didn't?

Of course I didn't.

Then what?

Then I went to the train station.

Was it busy, Snorri?

No. It was quiet. I was early. I stood on the platform and felt my toes go cold. But I didn't mind.

Because –

Because I was wearing the new socks that Mother had knitted for me.

Those blue ones?

Yes. You have a good memory.

Thank you.

So then the train came.

How many carriages did it have?

I don't know. Many. I got on. There were puddles on the floor and the carriage smelled of stale smoke.

Probably from cigarettes, Snorri.

Probably. I found a seat. The journey was pleasant.

What did you see?

Mainly the forest. Then mountains. Rivers. Villages. At certain points a road ran alongside the train tracks and there were cars on it and I could see the people behind the wheel and their children in the back seats and for a few moments it was like looking in a strange mirror, it was like seeing an alternative life, a life I could have lived had things been different, and then the train entered a tunnel and everything went dark. The suggestion of an alternative life was no more. The mirror disappeared.

Were you scared, Snorri?

Why would I be scared?

Dark.

I don't fear the dark.

Me neither. Sorry to interrupt.

That's OK. Every so often the train stopped and some people got off and some others got on, and then we would continue.

What did you do?

I stayed exactly where I was and I looked out the window. I was seeing our country for the first time.

Were you excited?

Excited, no. It was just how I expected it to look. I saw a lot of snow.

Did you speak to anyone on the train?

No, Frosti.

Not even the man who checked your train ticket?

We might have exchanged words. I don't recall.

What did he look like?

Again, I don't recall.

Then what?

We travelled some more. We passed a lake. We passed another lake. We entered a tunnel. We came out of the tunnel. A man came round with a trolley that sold hot drinks, snacks, that sort of thing.

What snacks?

Peanuts. Cheese and crackers. Fruit loaf. I think there was soup too.

What did you eat?

I had the cheese and crackers. They were dry.

All crackers are dry, Snorri.

Yes, but the cheese was dry too. And not in a good way. I wanted to ask for my money back but I knew that was not what you did. You just accepted it. We travelled some more.

Then you got to the city.

Then we got to the city. I had a map with me. I used the map to find my hotel. I went on foot.

Did it take a long time?

It seemed to take hours. The city was so busy. So noisy. Traffic was moving in all directions. Trams, cars, bicycles. There was a lot of excrement too.

Human?

No, dog. And the buildings. The buildings were so tall, like marble mountains.

What did you think about them?

I thought: What happens inside all these buildings?

And then?

And then I found the hotel, Frosti. It was on a side street. Trees were growing from between cracks in the pavement. There was a sort of shack outside that sold newspapers, chewing gum, chocolate bars, salt cod.

They have salt cod in the city too?

I think they have salt cod everywhere. I checked into my room.

Describe it.

It was big, but no bigger than our room. It had carpet. Thick carpet, with a pattern on it. The pattern I didn't much care for. It was OK. The mattress on the bed was soft and too high off the ground. There was a television in the room. It was nailed to the wall.

That's strange.

Very strange.

What else?

There was a table, a chair. A bathroom.

Did the toilet flush?

Yes. There was a shower too – it had both hot and cold water.

Imagine.

I took a shower.

Then what?

Then I got dressed and sat on the bed. It was dark outside but the city was noisy. There were car horns. Dogs barking. Voices. The man in the next room had his TV turned up loud.

Did you watch TV, Snorri?

I turned it on.

What did you watch?

Nothing of interest. I went downstairs.

You met a woman.

No. First I ate. I had a plate of sausages and cabbage in the dining room.

Was it nice?

The sausages needed more salt. The cabbage was acceptable.

Then you met a woman.

Then I went to the bar and ordered a beer.

Did it taste good?

No, Frosti. It tasted bad.

Why?

It left my mouth feeling dry and dusty. The gas made my stomach bloat like a drowned sheep. There was music playing. It was too loud.

The woman.

Yes. Then I got talking to a woman.

At the bar?

At the bar. She asked me to buy her a drink. I found this request rather forward, but you know me, Frosti. What I have I like to share.

You never have anything.

But when I do, I like to share it. I bought her a drink.

What drink?

Brandy, if I recall.

Brandy, Snorri!

Brandy. She talked, I listened.

Was she pretty?

She was OK.

Just OK?

Just OK.

What was she wearing?

I don't really remember.

Try.

Frosti, it was fifty years ago.

What did you talk about?

She talked a lot but I don't recall saying much. It was as if she was talking just to narrow the space between us; it was as if she was afraid of silence.

She must have been from the city.

Yes. She was from right there in the capital. She had a young son. The child's father wasn't around.

It's an increasingly common situation, Snorri.

Yes. But back then it was rarer. I told her I was a wood-cutter and that I lived at home with my brother and sister and she just nodded. Then she asked to see my room.

Why?

She said she wanted to see what it looked like.

Strange.

That's what I thought. We walked upstairs together.

Then she tried to kiss you.

Then she tried to kiss me.

What was it like?

Awkward. Her mouth pressed against mine like that. I can still smell the brandy and cigarettes on her. For some reason I thought of slugs and snails. Creatures of the sod.

What did you do?

What could I do? I just stood there and let her mouth keep on pressing until she'd had enough.

Is that when she asked you if you were one of them, Snorri?

Yes. That was when she asked me if I was *one of them*.

What did you say?

I said one of what?

And she said you know. One of *them*.

I said I have no idea what you mean. Then she got a little angry and said some things.

What things?

Bad things about people from the north country. Things about farmers and herdsmen and woodcutters. And animals too. I didn't appreciate her tone.

Then.

Then she asked me for money.

Why?

For payment.

Payment?

Yes, payment for her time.

For making you think of slugs and snails? The nerve of that woman, brother.

So then I asked her if she was one of them. And she said one of what? And I said you know, one of *them*.

And I bet she said I have no idea what you mean.

You're right, Frosti. That's exactly what she said. And she sneered as she said it too, and in that moment I saw all the ugliness of the city folk, the greed and the cynicism, and I asked her to leave or else I would call the manager of the hotel and tell him that *one of them* was in my room.

Good for you.

Well.

Well exactly, Snorri. What a to-do.

I know. It was the worst night of my life. I remember it like it was yesterday.

Me too.

But you weren't even there.

No, but I remember you telling me about it like it was yesterday.

. . .

Snorri.

Yes.

What was the woman called?

I never asked. All I remember is the name of the hotel. The Hotel Consort.

Do you ever wonder what the woman is doing today, Snorri?

No, Frosti. I don't.

———

I saw the fox prints again, Snorri.

When?

Yesterday.

By the medium log pile?

No. Right outside.

Out the back by the bin?

No. By our porch.

Was it the same one, do you think?

It's hard to say, Snorri. I like to think so.

That's the first time this year.

Yes. I hope she had cubs.

I think that's where she has been. In her den, tending to her young ones.

I like to think so. In some countries they hunt foxes, don't they.

So they say.

Why? There's no meat on them.

I don't know. People do the strangest things when they're bored.

I don't know how they find the time.

They chase them on horseback, with packs of dogs.

All that fuss over a fox that's doing no harm, Snorri?

I know. I saw something this morning too, Frosti.

What was that?

The men with the bright-coloured poles.

Where?

Here on the hillside. And over the other side of the valley too.

Was it the same men?

I don't know. But the poles were the same bright orange.

How many were there?

There were three men, Frosti. Two of them had poles. The other one had a device that stood on a tripod. He kept bending down to look at the men with the poles through it. The device was also orange. It looked like a square, stout telescope.

What could it mean?

They were surveyors, I think.

Surveyors?

Yes.

What were they doing?

They were surveying the valley.

But why, Snorri?

They were taking measurements. They were mapping the land.

I know what *surveying* means. But why were they doing it.

We had another letter, Frosti.

What letter?

I never mentioned it to you.

What letter?

Another one from that company.

The developers?

Yes.

The housing developers?

Yes, Frosti. The housing developers.

What did it say?

It said they wanted to help us realise the potential of the land.

What does that mean?

It said our cooperation would be greatly valued.

I still don't understand.

It said they wanted to reward us handsomely for our assets.

Our assets?

The land, Frosti. This land. Our house.

What would they want with our little house?

The same as they said in the first letter. It's not the cabin they are after, but the land. They have bought up all the space around us.

But why? There's nothing here but trees and hillside.

Exactly. It's the empty space they want.

Why?

To build houses on. Big houses for holiday homes.

Holiday homes. Why on earth would anyone want to come here on holiday?

Because it is beautiful, Frosti. And quiet.

I thought people would want to go to the sea or the city or get on an aeroplane to go on their holidays. Here there is nothing but frozen mud and snow, the stream and the pine trees.

The city folk like all that. And this company intends to provide it for them by building a resort here.

A resort.

Yes. A place with much bigger cabins, and roads, and shops and places to drink too much alcohol.

That doesn't sound good, Snorri.

No.

And the men with the orange poles – they are part of this?

Yes.

But I have been here for seventy-five years. You a little longer. What will we do?

I don't know. What do you want to do?

I don't want to do anything. I want to drink my coffee and then go and chop logs this afternoon. Later, when it is beginning to get dark, I will return and we will cook and eat.

Then that's what we shall do.

But what about the company with their letters and the men with their poles?

I don't know.

I don't think they're going to go away, Snorri.

I think the same.

The valley is all I know. The valley is all I want to know.

Yes, Frosti.

We are in the valley, but the valley is in us too.

Yes.

I want the men with the orange poles to go away and never come back.

Yes.

Tonight when I sleep I will dream them away.

OK, Frosti.

———

Well. Time to get chopping.

My mittens are still wet.

Take my spare pair.

Are you sure, Snorri?

It's fine. Mine are dry.

OK.

They are on the line.

This headache.

Still bad?

Yes.

Tonight I will make the stew, Frosti. You can take it easy.

I need to wash the socks.

The socks can wait.

And sweep.

Brother, the sweeping can wait also.

When I sweep I often think of Mother.

She was rarely without a broom in her hand.

She would follow you around the cabin.

Crumbs would fall from your bread and it seemed like they would hit the floor for only one second before she had swept them up.

Yes. She kept this place spotless. People would be judged on the cleanliness of their home. There were a lot of loose tongues in the valley about these things. Probably there still are.

I wonder what they say about us, Snorri?

Who cares.

Not me.

Me neither. We do alright.

Some days you could eat your dinner off our floor. Not that you'd want to.

Not that you'd want to, but you could.

Other days you would favour a plate.

That's the truth, brother.

Snorri.

Yes.

Do you think of Mother often?

I think of her sometimes. It has been a long time now.

Yes. Some days it feels like she is still here somewhere, watching us sweep and cook and clean. I can feel her.

I think this is quite natural.

Remember the laughs we had.

Yes, Frosti. These walls have seen good times.

You know what I was just thinking.

What?

I was thinking that maybe we should get some reindeer steaks for our Christmas table. Like we used to have.

No stew?

We could cook them liked Mother used to.

With the berries.

With the berries, the sauce, red cabbage.

Well, we could try, Frosti.

I can already taste it.

We should get back to the chopping, though.

If I close my eyes I can really taste it. Maybe I'll make gingerbread too.

We should get back to the chopping. Those mittens are on the line.

Thanks, Snorri. This afternoon when I chop I will think about venison and gingerbread and I will see you later.

III. TEA

My head still hurts, Snorri.

It will get better.

It may get worse.

Yes, it may get worse. But after, it will get better.

You don't know that for sure.

No. But it did last time.

Last time was different.

You always say that.

You don't know. You don't get headaches like I get headaches.

I get headaches.

Not like mine.

How would you know, Frosti?

Because if you did you would be complaining a lot more. You'd feel nauseous, irritable.

Maybe I just have a higher threshold for discomfort.

It's not discomfort – it's beyond that. It is pain that I am experiencing.

Well, maybe I have a higher threshold for pain, then.

I doubt that. I doubt that very much.

The only way to know would be if we both experienced the same level of pain at the same time. And then we would measure our reactions.

Like if we both cut our thumbs at the same time.

Yes. Something like that.

Like a blood brothers' pact?

Yes. But as we are already brothers, a blood pact would be unnecessary.

We could each chop a digit off. A little finger, perhaps. With the axe. I could do you, then you could do me. He who makes the most noise loses, Snorri.

Would it stop you complaining about your head?

It really hurts.

And then we'd both be without our little fingers.

I don't care. I'd do it.

To prove that your headache is real? I believe you, alright. I believe you.

The very fact that you're too scared suggests that you wouldn't be able to withstand pain like I can.

No. It just means I'm pragmatic, Frosti. More sensible. I value my little finger. You should too. We need them.

For what?

For many things.

Like what, for example?

Well, without them our hands would be twenty per cent less efficient, for example.

They're there for a reason.

. . .

. . .

Maybe you should lie down, Frosti?

If I lie down I get restless. Then I want to stand up and walk around.

So stand up, walk around.

But then I get dizzy.

So get some fresh air.

I don't want to put my boots on right now.

Go out barefoot, then. A good dose of frostbite might distract you from your headache.

You'd like that, wouldn't you?

You talk as if I celebrate your misfortune. I really don't. I'm just trying to make light of things, that's all. They say laughter is the best medicine.

Well, make me laugh, then. You've not said anything funny in a long time. You used to make me laugh a lot. Give me some of this famed medicine you speak of.

Well, what do you want me to say, Frosti?

I don't know.

I can't just come up with good humour off the top of my head.

Try.

Try?

Yes, try. Try and say something funny.

I can't think right now.

You're not the one with a headache, Snorri. At least have a go. This pain is intensifying.

Do you remember when we were boys and the pond froze over?

Of course.

And I threw your glove out into the middle and dared you to go and get it.

I remember.

And then the ice cracked and you got stuck up to your waist and I had to come and lasso the rope over your head like elk and then pull you out. That was pretty funny.

For you, maybe.

I still smile when I think about that now. The look on your face and the way you waved your arms about. But you always did carry a little more weight than me, Frosti.

I was wearing a thicker jerkin than you, that's all.

Well.

Is that the best you can do?

For now, yes.

Once again it is at the expense of my misfortune. I don't feel like laughing.

And your trousers froze as stiff as a young pine trunk on you. Do you remember?

Of course I do. Agna didn't laugh, though. Agna thought what you did was stupid and childish.

I was a child. Children do childish things.

And dangerous, Snorri.

Maybe it was a little dangerous. But it was the time of the spring thaw. You would have been fine for a good ten minutes.

Agna knew better. Agna didn't speak to you for the rest of the day.

I don't remember that part.

I do. She said I could have died and then what?

You wouldn't have died. I would have saved you, Frosti.

But you could have fallen through the ice too.

I could have, but I didn't.

But you could have.

What might have happened does not matter today. All that matters is what really happened. It was many, many years ago now.

I still remember it like it was yesterday.

Yes.

Agna was an angel, Snorri.

Yes. She was an angel.

I miss her.

I do too. But death is just a moment in time. How is your head feeling now?

Worse.

But after that it will get better.

That's easy for you to say.

Tomorrow we shall go into the village, says Snorri.

It is the weekend already?

Tomorrow it will be the weekend.

I don't know where the time goes, Snorri. What with the logs and the men with the orange poles and this headache, it is non-stop around here.

Yes. There is certainly never a dull moment.

The men with the orange poles are not helping my headache. I can't stop thinking about them.

Try not to, Frosti. You always were a worrier.

If they built big new houses and roads here, what would happen to the woods and the animals?

I don't know. The same as us, I suppose. They would be removed.

I don't want that to happen.

Me neither, Frosti.

We should make sure we never leave here.

Yes.

If we never leave then at least they cannot build on our land.

Yes.

Our father. He made this home for us with his own hands.

Yes.

They do not understand this, these men with their poles and letters.

No.

So let's never leave, Snorri.

OK, Frosti.

They'll have to fight the both of us.

OK, Frosti.

I like it here too much.

Me too.

And now the village is changing too, isn't it, Snorri?

Everything changes eventually.

They have the new bank. And the butcher's has closed. There is talk of a supermarket. Everything under one roof, they said – where is the sense in that?

I don't know, Frosti. Maybe that's what some people want.

We should do a list for tomorrow.

I know what we need to get. It will not differ from last week.

We need syrup. We didn't buy syrup last week and now we're nearly out.

So we'll get syrup.

We can't do without syrup.

I'm sure we'd live.

You might. But I think I'd die, Snorri.

Now you're being dramatic, Frosti.

Maybe a little. But I do like syrup.

I know. Ever since you were a small boy you have guzzled that stuff like it's water. You have a sweet tooth.

I just like syrup, is all.

I noticed.

We should get coffee too.

Yes.

And oats.

Of course.

And winter vegetables.

Frosti, I know all of this.

And our meat order.

. . .

And toothpaste. Got to look after your teeth, even if they are not your own.

. . .

And toilet paper. Not the cheap stuff this time. In these temperatures it feels like holly or something.

. . .

Snorri, I sense you are not listening to me.

I am listening. What I am not doing is speaking.

So now you're having one of your silent moods.

It's not a mood, I just have no reply. I know what we need to buy in the village, that is all. It doesn't change. It has not changed. Maybe we have to pick up something that we don't consume in one week, maybe we don't. There is a little variation here and there, but mainly our supplies have stayed the same for years. Certainly since we lost Agna twenty-five long years ago.

It feels like yesterday.

Yes.

Dear Agna. She was a better cook than both of us.

That is true, brother.

We just eat because we need to eat, but Agna – Agna really knew how to make a mutton stew.

Seasoning. She really had a great grasp on seasoning. It makes a difference, Frosti.

What she didn't know about the preservation of whale steak was not worth knowing. And remember her meatballs, Snorri. The way they just fell apart in your mouth like that? A little kale on the side.

My mouth is watering, little brother.

Mine too.

. . .

. . .

———

Let me ask you a question, Snorri.

Go on.

Which one of us do you think will go first?

Go?

Die, I mean.

Now, Frosti. What sort of a question is that to ask on a day like this. Haven't we got enough to think about, what with the snow and the logs and the men with their poles, and don't forget tomorrow's shopping. I told you to stop thinking so much.

Yes, I know. But still.

But still what?

Which one of us do you think will die first?

That won't be for a long time, Frosti.

Today I feel old, Snorri. This headache –

Your headache will pass.

. . .

Headaches don't last forever, Frosti. You are just feeling a little off colour today, that is all. I know what you are like. You dwell upon these things. You worry too much, little brother.

Maybe. I can't help it. It's just all this talk of holiday resorts has me thinking. We won't live forever, Snorri.

We might.

We won't.

I know we won't, but why worry about it? Think about your sweat lodge. Sometimes it pays to concentrate on things you look forward to.

It will be a great sweat lodge.

Yes.

As soon as the spring thaw comes you must build it, says Snorri.

But you said it was just another of my winter dreams.

Dreams can become a reality. I have confidence in you, Frosti.

You're just saying that because you want a turn in my sweat lodge.

Maybe. Maybe not.

You never answered my question, Snorri.

Which question?

The one about which one of us will go first.

I am not answering that question. It is a silly question. How can we know?

We can't know. I'm just wondering.

Well, you shouldn't. All that wondering and thinking and dreaming gives you headaches. Me, I chop and I stack and I walk and I work, but I do not speculate about what might or might not be. And I remain headache-free. Do you see the point that I am making, Frosti?

Yes. I see the point that you are making.

How is your head now?

I don't know. A little better, maybe.

Good.

It's hard to tell. I feel it behind my eyeball.

Stop thinking about death. And drink some water.

I drank some water.

Drink some more water and drown the headache.

Is that a saying? Drink some more water and drown the headache?

No. I just made it up now.

Oh.

Now. I should get this stew on the go.

What are we having, Snorri?

Ham hock and vegetable.

My favourite.

Could you pass the ham from the cold room?

Of course.

While you do that I'll chop these vegetables.

Here you go.

Thanks. This knife needs sharpening.

Perhaps we can take it with us tomorrow and get it done in the village.

Yes. That's a good idea. It's about as blunt as these carrots.

Do you ever tire of stew, Snorri?

What a question to ask.

Well, do you?

I never give it any thought. Why – do you?

No. As you know, I like it a lot.

Good.

Of course, sometimes I like to eat fish.

Well, me too. But you know that we are out of salt fish, Frosti.

Yes.

We finished the last barrel in September.

Yes.

Perhaps we can get some more.

I'd like that. I could make us salt fish fritters.

I like your salt fish fritters, Frosti.

The secret is to drain the fish for forty-eight hours, mix them with cornflour if you can get it, then fry them in butter. I like to serve them with kale.

Me too. Kale is good. Kale is full of iron.

You know, this afternoon I had a nosebleed.

A nosebleed?

Yes, Snorri.

What happened?

I'm not sure that anything happened. I was standing for a moment having a rest and I felt something strange in my forehead.

What do you mean?

Just like something popped inside.

Popped?

Yes. Like my brain was relaxing. And then the air seemed to be suddenly very sharp in my nose. Like ice. I could smell it. Then I sneezed and drops of blood splattered the snow. I put my hand to my nose and it was bleeding.

Did it hurt at all, Frosti?

No. It didn't hurt. It felt fine. Like I was being unblocked or unburdened of something. It almost felt good.

Good?

Like a relief.

Maybe you banged your nose while chopping.

No. Not at all. Then more blood came. Some ran on to my lip and I licked at it and the taste took me right back to that time.

Which time?

That time we were sledging at Devil's Nape, Snorri.

I don't remember.

Sure you do. We were sledging and some boys from the village came over. One of them pushed me off my sledge and took it.

I don't recall, Frosti.

It was the big sledge that Father made. The one with the metal runners. Then one of the other boys threw a snowball with a rock in it that hit me. It hit me square on the head and I heard bells ringing. I bit into my tongue.

Wait. I think I remember.

You went up to the boy who threw the snowball at me. You didn't run and you didn't act angry. You just walked over to him. He was laughing. He was taller than you. Much taller. And thin too. I was around ten so you must have been twelve, thirteen.

Those two years make a difference at that age, Frosti.

They do.

I can picture him now. Did something happen?

Yes.

Did I hit him?

Yes. You hit him. You hit him hard, Snorri. You could barely reach his face but one punch was all it took. His nose exploded. I remember the blood. The way it landed on the snow. A flash of red on the landscape. It was like I was seeing the colour for the first time. True red, I mean. So bright. So shocking. Then the snow soaked it up, diluted it.

Then what?

Then the boy ran off crying. His friend who had stolen my sledge walked back up the hill and gave it back to me. He looked scared of you. He apologised and said he had only been kidding around. He said he didn't mean any harm.

We later become friends, me and him.

You did?

Yes. At school. I forget his name. He was OK. The boy I hit I never much liked.

I wonder what became of him.

He died young.

Is that true, Snorri?

That is true, Frosti.

How did he die?

I don't recall. He had a disease. He was in his twenties. Maybe it was his liver. Or maybe it was his lungs. He worked in a factory, that is all I know.

I was proud to have you as my brother that day, Snorri. The way you stuck up for me.

It was nothing. He was a bully. You were my little brother.

Still. He was a lot bigger than you.

It just means he had further to fall, that's all.

Well.

Well.

The nosebleed today. It reminded me of this.

You have a good memory.

You have a good right hook.

Thanks.

I can picture the boy now. The look on his face when you hit him.

Well, what did he expect, throwing rocks at kids.

I think he learned a lesson that day, Snorri.

Maybe. But even after that he would still bully other kids.

He did?

Yes. I don't think he learned that much.

He never bothered us again, though, did he.

That's true. It's such a long time ago.

Must be sixty-five years. A different century.

Frosti, how is your headache now?

My headache is still there.

Did your nosebleed last very long?

It bled for a long time. Then I rubbed snow on my nose and my face and that seemed to help. Then I carried on chopping.

The air feels thin today. Rarefied.

Maybe that's it. Maybe that's why I had a nosebleed. I never have nosebleeds.

Me neither.

I couldn't stop staring at the blood. The pattern it made in the snow. In a strange way it was pretty.

Blood is such an unexpected colour. Nowhere else in nature do you see that colour. Not in berries, not in the breast of a bird. Only inside us does that red exist. Then when it comes we are surprised by the shock of its beauty.

That's very well put, Snorri.

But it's true.

Well.

Well.

———

Did I ever tell you what my name means?

Snorri, you mean?

Yes.

Sure. It means snow. Frosti is frost and you're snow. And Agna meant goodness, purity. Chastity.

Well, that's where you are wrong, little brother.

I think you'll find I'm right.

On your name, yes. And maybe Agna too. Frosti is indeed Old Norse for frost. An ancient name in use across Scandinavia. But Snorri – Snorri is purely an Icelandic name. Less a Norse name and more one that specifically comes from that treeless island. It means hard fighting. Father named me after a character in the Sagas. Snorri the unmentionable.

Snorri the Unmentionable? What sort of a name is that?

His name wasn't Snorri the Unmentionable, Frosti. It was Snorri – the something-I-don't-care-to-say.

I don't understand.

A rude word.

Snorri the rude word.

Yes.

What word?

Do I have to spell it out for you.

I'm interested. You brought up the subject.

It's Bastard, Frosti.

Snorri the Bastard?

Yes.

You were named after someone called Snorri the Bastard?

Yes. A hard-fighting warrior of the old Sagas.

You were named after a hard-fighting warrior of the old Sagas called Snorri the Bastard, Agna was named for her virtuosity and big heart, and I was named after frozen water vapour.

Yes. That appears to be the case, Frosti.

I'm not sure how I feel about that. All my life I thought of you and I as frost and snow. Two variants of the same thing.

It's not the case. Not in name, anyway.

I see that now.

Yes.

Wow. Snorri the Bastard.

Yes.

Have you read the Sagas, Snorri?

You know I'm not much of a reader, Frosti.

Well, me neither.

Books are for other people.

So having not read the Sagas, we don't even know this to be true.

It's what Uncle Ulf told me.

And you believed him!

I had no reason not to.

Apart from the fact that he was the most famous teller of tall tales in the whole valley, Snorri. Uncle Ulf. They called him Pinocchio for a reason, you know. Snorri the Bastard. Honestly. There's no such character, brother.

I believe there to be.

Well. I bet the smell of liquor was strong on his breath and his eyes a little glassy when he told you this, no?

I don't know, Frosti. I just like the story about the fighting warrior.

So like the story – and be a warrior. After all, you felled that boy like a giant Canadian redwood all those years ago. But don't go telling people you're named after a character that doesn't even exist. Tongues will wag.

Well.

I do miss Uncle Ulf. He was fun.

Yes. He was. He was well liked. You know, Frosti, he was only fifty when he fell in the snow that night and never got up.

Fifty?

Yes. A quarter-century younger than you are now, Frosti. It took three days for him to thaw out.

I remember. They said it was the first bath he'd had since they put a man on the moon.

Putting a man on the moon would have been easier than getting Uncle Ulf to take a bath.

That's true, Snorri. What was it that Uncle Ulf did? For a living, I mean?

He drained vodka bottles for a vodka company.

He was good at his job, though, wasn't he?

Yes, he was. He was indeed. The very best. He had many years of practice.

He was not like Father.

No. He was not. Father never touched a drop. Except at New Year.

Everyone touches a drop at New Year. I'll be taking a drop myself.

They say his liver was like reindeer pâté at the end. How is your headache now, Frosti?

It is like a steel balaclava.

That bad?

That bad. It hurts to blink. And now my jaw aches too.

Remember when Uncle Ulf fell off the roof while tarring it?

Of course. That's how he got his limp.

And his stutter.

Yes. And his stutter. That was when he took to the drinking.

Oh, he had already started on that, little brother.

He had?

Yes.

Uncle Ulf.

Yes. What a character. A rare beast, that one. Do you know what the name Ulf means?

No, Snorri. Tell me.

I have no idea.

I think maybe it means buffoon.

You could be right there, Frosti. You could be right.

———

I think I might turn in early tonight.

You're not going to have coffee?

No, Snorri. Not tonight. It's this headache. It feels like an icicle has fallen from the frozen waterfall and pierced my head. The pain is cold and the pain is sharp. It's a distraction.

I can put another log on the burner. I've been saving a special one.

That's OK.

Well, if you're sure.

I'm sure.

Tomorrow is another day, little brother. Your head will be better.

I hope so.

And if it is not I will walk down to the village and pick up the supplies myself.

How will you manage?

I'll manage.

But you'll never be able to carry them all, Snorri. What about my syrup?

Don't worry. I'll find a way. I'll get you your syrup.

Without syrup I might die.

There you go again. Exaggerating.

Maybe a little.

You are like a child sometimes, Frosti.

Yes.

Sometimes I forget we are old men.

Yes.

You make me feel young.

That's good. That's good. I'm glad I make you feel young, Snorri.

It's not so bad.

It could be worse.

It could always be worse.

Well.

Well.

I'll turn in, then.

I'm going to sit in front of the burner for a while longer.

OK.

Maybe watch the snow for a while.

It's really falling again.

Yes. Like ashes from an extinguished sun.

There will be deep drifts tomorrow.

Yes.

We'll need to clear them.

Yes.

At this rate they'll be over the front porch.

Don't worry about that, Frosti. There will always be snow. There will always be drifts. But there will always be shovels too.

But there won't always be us.

No.

Well. Snorri, the men with the orange poles –

Sleep deep, Frosti.

OK. I will.

Goodnight.

———

I heard the geese in the night again, Frosti. They arrived right on time. First one V-formation, then another. Then shortly after that, two more. I could hear their honking from a long way off. It echoed right down the valley. It was very loud but by the time they reached us they were silent. I think perhaps they were saving their energy for the long flight ahead. They flew so low I could hear the flap of their wings right above our roof. I could hear the wind in their feathers, the rasp of their lungs. It sounded like magic. Did you hear them, Frosti?

. . .

We are right under their flight path. Every year they come, right on time. For many years now. Generations. And every year I hear their honking echoing down the valley, and it wakes me just in time to hear them pass over us. When I was a boy I thought the noise was that of a mythical sky beast passing over us. You always slept through it, Frosti, and when you woke up and I told you about the noise the mythical sky beast made you didn't believe me. You thought I was making it all up. Then one morning Father told me that it wasn't a beast, but geese in flight. He said they always fly together, in small V-shaped groups, and they take it in turns to lead. I found that idea even more exciting than the one my imagination had made up. Father also said that when the geese migrate they fly three thousand miles. That fact staggered me. I have only ever travelled three hundred miles and as you know that was for one disappointing night. You, little brother, have travelled even less. I don't recall you ever going more than thirty miles. You never did like to leave the valley. And now we are old men.

. . .

Well, anyway, I suspect our travelling days are over, Frosti. Some weeks the three miles into town feels a lot longer. These snowdrifts don't help. There was another heavy fall in the night. I can feel it. See how it lightens the room. Hear how it muffles the call of the dawn birds. It surely lies thick this morning; I think that walking will be a trial today. Two steps in snow is like twenty in grass. But why travel when the world just on your doorstep changes every day? That thing about every snowflake being different. Well. To me every day is different, little brother. We may drink our coffee and eat our oats, but no two skies are the same. No two trees are the same. Or people. And each dream we have is different from the last.

. . .

Do you hear me, Frosti?

. . .

I bet he is dreaming now.

. . .

Dreaming of syrup, probably.

. . .

Or that sweat lodge.

. . .

Frosti?

. . .

It is nearly time to get up, Frosti.

. . .

Frosti.

. . .

Frosti.

. . .

. . .

. . .

Notes

Some of these stories were inspired by real incidents and real people, though artistic licence has been applied to varying degrees throughout.

'A Thousand Acres of English Soil' was runner-up in the Society of Authors' Tom-Gallon Trust Award 2018. 'The Folk Song Singer' won the Society of Authors' Tom-Gallon Trust Award 2014. It was published as a download-only 'double A-side' release as part of Galley Beggar Press's Singles Club.

'An English Ending', 'The Museum of Extinct Animals' and 'Old Ginger' were first published by Somesuch Stories between 2015 and 2017. 'The Museum of Extinct Animals' also featured in the *Somesuch Stories Volume 1* print anthology, published in 2015.

'The Whip Hand' was published in 2018 as a single chapbook, limited to fifty-three signed and numbered copies as part of the Walking Wounded Series by Tangerine Press. 'The Bloody Bell' was originally commissioned by

Hexham Book Festival 2016 for their Mansio project, and written during a week's residency near Hadrian's Wall. An extended version of the story appeared in their collection, *The Mansio: New Writing Inspired by Hadrian's Wall* (Hexham Book Festival, 2016).

'Ten Men' was written for the International Literature Showcase 2017, through the National Centre for Writing. It also appeared in print in *The New Issue* in 2020.

'Snorri & Frosti' was first published in 2013 as a downloadable story as part of Galley Beggar Press's Singles Club. It was also published as a limited-edition chapbook by 3:AM Books in 2014.

Acknowledgements

Thank you to Kathryn Myers for her input. My agents, Jessica Woollard, Clare Israel and Alice Howe, and all at David Higham Associates. My editor, Angelique Tran Van Sang, Terry Lee, Allegra Le Fanu and all at Bloomsbury. Thanks also to Alexa von Hirschberg.

I also extend gratitude to the following editors: Susie Troup. Will Atkins. Eloise Millar and Sam Jordison. Susan Tomaselli, Christiana Spens and Andrew Gallix. Suze Olbrich and Sharon O'Connell. Michael Curran. Antonia Charlesworth and Kevin Gopal. Adam Pugh. The Society of Authors. Love and respect: Cally Callomon, Gabrielle Drake and Shane Meadows.

And thank you to Adelle Stripe and my family and friends.

ALSO AVAILABLE BY BENJAMIN MYERS

THE OFFING

An *Observer* Pick for 2019

One summer following the Second World War, Robert Appleyard sets out on foot from his Durham village. Sixteen and the son of a coal miner, he makes his way across the northern countryside until he reaches the former smuggling village of Robin Hood's Bay. There he meets Dulcie, an eccentric, worldly, older woman who lives in a ramshackle cottage facing out to sea.

Staying with Dulcie, Robert's life opens into one of rich food, sea-swimming, sunburn and poetry. The two come from different worlds, yet as the summer months pass, they form an unlikely friendship that will profoundly alter their futures.

'A shift in direction . . . but one that has paid off gloriously in this intense and evocative novel that brings to mind JL Carr's *A Month in the Country*' Alex Preston, *Observer*, Picks for 2019

'Powerful, visceral writing, historical fiction at its best. Benjamin Myers is one to watch' Pat Barker

'In his element, Myers is thrilling: intelligent, dangerous and near untouchable' *New Statesman*

ORDER YOUR COPY:
BY PHONE: +44 (0) 1256 302 699
BY EMAIL: DIRECT@MACMILLAN.CO.UK
DELIVERY IS USUALLY 3–5 WORKING DAYS.
FREE POSTAGE AND PACKAGING FOR ORDERS OVER £20.
ONLINE: WWW.BLOOMSBURY.COM/BOOKSHOP
PRICES AND AVAILABILITY SUBJECT TO CHANGE WITHOUT NOTICE.

BLOOMSBURY.COM/AUTHOR/BENJAMIN-MYERS

B L O O M S B U R Y

THE GALLOWS POLE

Winner of the 2018 Walter Scott Prize and
a Roger Deakin Award

From his remote moorland home, David Hartley assembles a gang of weavers and land-workers to embark upon a criminal enterprise that will capsize the economy and become the biggest fraud in British history. They are the Cragg Vale Coiners and their business is 'clipping' – the forging of coins, a treasonous offence punishable by death. When an excise officer vows to bring them down and with the industrial age set to change the face of England forever, Hartley's empire begins to crumble. Forensically assembled, *The Gallows Pole* is a true story of resistance and a rarely told alternative history of the North.

'One of my books of the year ... It's the best thing Myers has done' Robert Macfarlane, *Big Issue* Books of the Year

'A windswept, brutal tale of eighteenth-century Yorkshire told in starkly beautiful prose' *Guardian*

'A brutal tale told with an original, muscular voice' *The Times*

ORDER YOUR COPY:
BY PHONE: +44 (0) 1256 302 699
BY EMAIL: DIRECT@MACMILLAN.CO.UK
DELIVERY IS USUALLY 3–5 WORKING DAYS.
FREE POSTAGE AND PACKAGING FOR ORDERS OVER £20.
ONLINE: WWW.BLOOMSBURY.COM/BOOKSHOP
PRICES AND AVAILABILITY SUBJECT TO CHANGE WITHOUT NOTICE.

BLOOMSBURY.COM/AUTHOR/BENJAMIN-MYERS

B L O O M S B U R Y

BEASTINGS

Winner of the Portico Prize for Literature and
the Northern Writers' Award

A girl and a baby. A priest and a poacher. A savage pursuit through the landscape
of a changing rural England.

When a teenage girl leaves the workhouse and abducts a child placed in her
care, the local priest is called upon to retrieve them. Chased through the
Cumbrian mountains of a distant past, the girl fights starvation and the elements,
encountering the hermits, farmers and hunters who occupy the remote hillside
communities. An American Southern Gothic tale set against the violent beauty
of Northern England, *Beastings* is a sparse and poetic novel about morality,
motherhood and corruption.

'Intimate and elemental ... Myers has the potential to become a true tragedian
of the fells' *Guardian*

'This bitter, alarming, occasionally visionary novel of the British wilderness is
likely to linger in the mind for some time' *New Statesman*

'Myers is quite simply an excellent and already accomplished writer. His prose is
taut, confident, professionally polished but at the same time maintaining a sense
of rustic and unrefined authenticity, that which is truly hewn' Sarah Hall

ORDER YOUR COPY:
BY PHONE: +44 (0) 1256 302 699
BY EMAIL: DIRECT@MACMILLAN.CO.UK
DELIVERY IS USUALLY 3–5 WORKING DAYS.
FREE POSTAGE AND PACKAGING FOR ORDERS OVER £20.
ONLINE: WWW.BLOOMSBURY.COM/BOOKSHOP
PRICES AND AVAILABILITY SUBJECT TO CHANGE WITHOUT NOTICE.

BLOOMSBURY.COM/AUTHOR/BENJAMIN-MYERS

BLOOMSBURY

PIG IRON

Winner of the Gordon Burn Prize

John-John wants to escape his past. But the legacy of brutality left by his boxer father, King of the Gypsies, Mac Wisdom, overshadows his life. His new job as an ice cream man should offer freedom, but instead pulls him into the dark recesses of a northern town where his family name is mud. When he attempts to trade prejudice and parole officers for the solace of the rural landscape, Mac's bloody downfall threatens John-John's very survival.

'*Pig Iron* is an important book because it tells a story that has shaped all contemporary Western humans, but is routinely, inexplicably overlooked – the great move from agricultural life to industrial life. The respect in which that shapes human culture and individual humans' Deborah Orr

'His poetic vernacular brims with that quality most sadly lost – humanity' *Guardian*

'One of my best reads this year ... A deeply rural story, a book full of passion for the English countryside and centred on the conflict between the travelling and the settled community. A very fine read indeed, it expresses a life view almost never examined in our narrow literary culture' Melvin Burgess

ORDER YOUR COPY:
BY PHONE: +44 (0) 1256 302 699
BY EMAIL: DIRECT@MACMILLAN.CO.UK
DELIVERY IS USUALLY 3–5 WORKING DAYS.
FREE POSTAGE AND PACKAGING FOR ORDERS OVER £20.
ONLINE: WWW.BLOOMSBURY.COM/BOOKSHOP
PRICES AND AVAILABILITY SUBJECT TO CHANGE WITHOUT NOTICE.

BLOOMSBURY.COM/AUTHOR/BENJAMIN-MYERS

BLOOMSBURY

A Note on the Type

The text of this book is set Adobe Garamond. It is one of several versions of Garamond based on the designs of Claude Garamond. It is thought that Garamond based his font on Bembo, cut in 1495 by Francesco Griffo in collaboration with the Italian printer Aldus Manutius. Garamond types were first used in books printed in Paris around 1532. Many of the present-day versions of this type are based on the *Typi Academiae* of Jean Jannon cut in Sedan in 1615.

Claude Garamond was born in Paris in 1480. He learned how to cut type from his father and by the age of fifteen he was able to fashion steel punches the size of a pica with great precision. At the age of sixty he was commissioned by King Francis I to design a Greek alphabet, and for this he was given the honourable title of royal type founder. He died in 1561.